Presented to:

HE ENJOYS TRUE LEISURE WHO HAS
TIME *to* IMPROVE HIS SOUL'S ESTATE.
Henry David Thoreau

PRESENTED BY:

DATE:

Beach Prayers

A Vacation *for* Your Soul

HONOR **HB** BOOKS

Inspiration and Motivation for the Seasons of Life

COOK COMMUNICATIONS MINISTRIES
Colorado Springs, Colorado • Paris, Ontario
KINGSWAY COMMUNICATIONS LTD
Eastbourne, England

Honor Books® is an imprint of
Cook Communications Ministries, Colorado Springs, CO 80918
Cook Communications, Paris, Ontario
Kingsway Communications Ltd., Eastbourne, England

BEACH PRAYERS: A VACATION FOR YOUR SOUL
Copyright © 2007 HONOR BOOKS

First printing, 2007
Printed in Canada

Manuscript written and compiled by Rebecca Currington, Vicki J. Kuyper, Patricia Mitchell, Julie
Sutton in association with SnapdragonGroup℠ Editorial Services
Cover Design: Greg Jackson, Thinkpen Design, LLC
Cover Photo: © iStockPhoto
Interior Design: Sandy Flewelling, TrueBlue Design
Interior Art: Drawings © Jupiter Images; Backgrounds © Harold Fila and © Ali Mazraie Shadi;
Decorative elements © Chris Ruch and © Sandy Flewelling

ISBN 978-1-56292-830-8

Contents

Introduction

VACATION MEANS TIME AWAY. Time for rest, renewal, a break from responsibility. Time to settle back and realign your physical, mental, emotional, and spiritual center of gravity. No wonder so many people choose to spend their vacations at the beach, where water, sand, sun, and endless horizons come together. It's a natural!

Beach Prayers: A Vacation for Your Soul was written expressly to inspire your vacation, whether you're reading from the comfort of your living-room sofa or sitting in a beach chair gazing out at the waves. You'll find fascinating meditations on life, encouragement from God's Word, inspiring quotes, and heartfelt prayers to put everything in perspective. We hope this unpretentious volume will give you the friendly little push you need to make these insights real in your life.

It's going to be a hot one, so don't forget the sunscreen—and God bless you as you read, relax, and just "be."

I WILL REFRESH THE WEARY
and SATISFY THE FAINT.

Jeremiah 31:25

Lean Back and Relax

YOU PEER INTO THE SHALLOW waves lapping against your slightly sunburned knees. Through the water you see a shifting landscape. Waves of sand undulate back and forth with the rhythmic surge of the sea. Pebbles, shells, and bits of coral dance around ten toes—your own—resting on the ocean's sandy floor. Is there anything about this scene that would lead you to believe you could float on the surface of the sea?

Rocks sink. Shells sink. Even minuscule grains of sand, after being playfully churned in the pull of the tides, eventually come to rest on the bottom of the sea. Yet the water that pours so easily through your fist can be trusted to keep your body afloat, regardless of what size swimsuit you wear. But that doesn't make resting your weight on something that isn't solid (and that people have been known to drown in!) easy.

Learning to float involves taking a risk. The only way you can learn to trust that the sea will support you is by putting it to the test. You don't need to understand the physics behind why you can float. You don't have to be totally doubt-free before you get in the water. What you need to do is lean back, relax, and let the sea simply do what it was created to do.

One thing you were created to do is trust in God. However, not everything you see will seem to support this truth. That's because human eyes can't always detect an almighty hand at work. But you don't have to understand the "why" of God's ways before you choose to trust in the "who" that's behind them. The more you risk leaning on God, resting your life in his hands instead of relying solely on your own resources and abilities, the more trustworthy you'll find he is—and the more at home you'll feel in the endless ocean of his love.

Blessed is the man who trusts in the Lord, whose confidence is in him. He will be like a tree planted by the water that sends out its roots by the stream. It does not fear when heat comes; its leaves are always green. It has no worries in a year of drought and never fails to bear fruit.
Jeremiah 17:7–8

You will keep in perfect peace him whose mind is steadfast, because he trusts in you. Trust in the LORD forever, for the LORD, the LORD, is the Rock eternal.
Isaiah 26:3–4

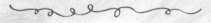

TRUST IS ONE OF THE FUNDAMENTAL ASPECTS OF LIFE *for* EVERY HUMAN EXISTENCE. ONLY TRUST ALLOWS THE SOUL ROOM TO BREATHE.
Wolfhart Pannenberg

Dear Lord: My soul is replenished as I wait on you. Renew my strength as I place my whole trust in your loving-kindness and faithfulness. Teach me to relax in the safety of your everlasting arms. Amen.

Soul Songs

As you survey the calm waters of a secluded ocean inlet, you notice a burst of misty spray. Next, the sight of a fin or tail breaking the surface of the sea catches your eye. But it's what follows that leaves you breathless with awe. A humpback whale catapults toward the sky, then quickly falls sideways back into the turquoise bay. Close to sixty-four tons make a gargantuan splash.

The humpback is more than just the acrobat of the whale family. It's also the lead vocalist. Their "songs" can last a few minutes to over an hour and can be heard up to one hundred miles away. Each whale has its own unique vocal signature, its own identifiable voice.

So do you. God knows your voice, from your softest sigh to your loudest cry. When you call out to him, he isn't distracted by the other "songs in the sea." You have his full attention, anytime, anywhere, from the depths of your struggles to your mountaintop highs. And although God could still hear you from one hundred miles away, he never strays that far. He's always by your side. Ever present. Ever loving. Ever listening.

Every prayer is like a song, complete with a tune and a theme. Its emotional tune may vary from joy to grief, confusion to awe, doubt to trust. Its theme will be determined by your current needs, concerns, and questions. In the same way that humpbacks often sing the same songs over and over again, God invites you to do the same. He never gets bored or impatient with what you have to say. He wants you to share what's on your heart—what you think, what you feel, what's important to you today.

Why not sing a heartfelt song to God right now? Your prayers, and your unique voice, are music to his ears.

The prayer of the upright is [God's] delight.
Proverbs 15:8 KJV

*The eyes of the LORD are on the righteous and
his ears are attentive to their prayer.*
1 Peter 3:12

Delight yourself in the LORD and he will give you the desires of your heart.
Psalm 37:4

LET YOUR JOYFUL HEART PRAISE *and* MAGNIFY
SO GOOD AND GLORIOUS A CREATOR.
William Law

Dear Lord: My prayer to you is so often encumbered with cares and concerns. Today I come to you focused only on you—your goodness, your kindness, your mercy, your grace. I lift my voice in praise to you. Hear the song my heart is singing and make it worthy of your presence. Amen.

Better Safe Than Sunburned

 WHEN IT COMES TO SPENDING a day at the beach, you're probably familiar with the drill:

- *Apply sunscreen with an SPF of at least 15, even when it's overcast; then reapply every two hours.*
- *Never swim alone.*
- *If you're caught in a riptide, don't try to swim against it; float with it until you find a break in the current where you can swim safely back to shore.*
- *Drink plenty of water.*
- *Never touch a jellyfish.*

A beautiful beach, bathed in sunshine and rimmed by the golden sands of a powdery shore, is often depicted as paradise. But even what we think of as paradise isn't problem-free. It can be a perilous place. That doesn't mean you should shun the wonders of the shoreline or spend your vacation consumed by fear. By following a few simple rules, you can protect yourself from potential danger so you can relax and enjoy the day ahead.

What's true for your body is also true for your soul. There are dangers along the way. The Bible says that you have an enemy who "prowls around like a roaring lion looking for someone to devour" (1 Peter 5:8). Sounds ominous, like a shark in lion's clothing. But Scripture also says there's spiritual armor available (see Eph. 6) that will not only protect you but will also make your enemy hightail it the other way.

At the beach you arm yourself with sunscreen and water wings. Your soul also needs protective gear, such as truth, righteousness, faith, the Word of God, and prayer. Just as the right scuba-diving equipment protects a diver from harm during a dive, this protective gear will keep you safe and spiritually sound as you venture deeper into the abundant life God has planned for you.

So let us put aside the deeds of darkness and put on the armor of light.
Romans 13:12

I am an example to many people, because you are my strong protection.
I am always praising you; all day long I honor you.
Psalm 71:7–8 NCV

SECURITY IS NOT THE ABSENCE *of* DANGER, BUT
THE PRESENCE OF GOD, NO MATTER WHAT THE DANGER.
Anne Ortlund

Heavenly Father: Each moment of each day, I feel your arms protecting me, steering me away from danger and out of harm's way. Remind me to put on the protective gear you've provided for me—truth, righteousness, faith, your Word, and prayer. Even that I can't do alone. I need your hand to guide me, your heart to direct my soul. Amen.

The Journey of Beach Glass

THE CRASHING WAVES ARE RELENTLESS. The pounding surf tumbles you in the salty sea, then tosses you onto the rocky shore. Capriciously, the tide pulls you back into the water to pummel you again and again. It seems as though the world as you've known it is near an end.

You entered the sea transparent, jagged, a mere chip of a bottle carelessly tossed aside after a picnic on the beach. But with the passing of time, you've undergone a transformation, a rebirth. Today a young child plucks you from a tide pool with eager fingers, brushing bits of sand from the subtle craters that now adorn your once bottle-glass-smooth exterior. She turns you over once, twice, admiring the opaque frost that has colored you the hue of springtime snow. You've become a treasure in her pocket, a velvety touchstone she fingers when she's bored, a secret gem she stores in her jewelry box, a precious gift from the sea.

When you find yourself in the midst of crashing waves and pounding tides, it's hard to believe that anything good could come out of so much pain and strife. But God is a God of wonders. He uses everything, including hardship and suffering, to help you mature into the uniquely beautiful creation you were designed to be. The process itself isn't pleasant. But in the same way athletes push themselves beyond what they think they can do to become stronger, faster, more skilled competitors, adversity can bring out the best in you—if you let it.

When storm clouds gather and the waves begin to churn, don't panic. Use God's presence and promises as your life preserver. Cling to the knowledge that he is near. Turn to him for strength, peace, and perspective. And anticipate that something of rare beauty will be revealed in you as a result of the adversity you face.

Blessed is the man who perseveres under trial, because when he has stood the test, he will receive the crown of life that God has promised to those who love him.
James 4:12

I consider that our present sufferings are not worth comparing with the glory that will be revealed in us.
Romans 8:18

ADVERSITY CAN EITHER DESTROY *or* BUILD UP, DEPENDING ON OUR CHOSEN RESPONSE.
Tim Hansel

Heavenly Father: All I've been able to think about is escaping from this trial I've been living with. Honestly, I just want it to be over. But I also want to learn as much as I can, gain as much from this uncomfortable situation as possible. I guess I'm trying to say that I don't want to waste any of my suffering. So I lift it up to you. Teach me in the midst of the crashing waves. Use this adversity to make me what you created me to be. Amen.

Unseen Allies

LAZING IN THE SAND, eyes closed, you've been lulled into half sleep by the repetitive slosh of the surf, when an unknown visitor crosses between you and the sun. The cool brush of a shadow grazes your cheek, pulling you back toward full consciousness. Opening your eyes, you notice a flock of seabirds heading toward the distant shore. They dip and glide like a feathered cloud sashaying across the afternoon sky. Their freedom from an earthbound existence stirs something deep in your soul. You long to join them, to sail high above the waves, to look down on the earth below, to ride the air currents with angelic grace.

The image most people hold in their mind's eye of what angels are like is a kind of ethereal, altruistic creature—part human, part avian. But the angels the Bible describes are neither flesh nor fowl. They have two, four, or six wings. Some have four faces: that of a lion, an ox, an eagle, and a man. They're warriors, messengers, and comforters, so gloriously fearsome in appearance that often the first words they utter to those they encounter on earth are "Fear not!" God created them to serve him—and his children. That includes you.

Though most people will never encounter an angel face-to-face in this life, or even feel the shadow of its wings, angels are as real as God himself. They're part of what's going on behind the scenes in this world, a spiritual scenario in which you, too, play a part. They're as different from you as you are from a seabird, but your love and worship of God binds you together with a common purpose. You're working together as God's representatives in this world. So fear not. God has provided you with some powerful allies who are fighting for you when life feels like anything but a day at the beach.

> *The angel of the LORD guards all who fear him,*
> *and he rescues them.*
> Psalm 34:7 NLT

> *God will command his angels to protect*
> *you wherever you go.*
> Psalm 91:11 CEV

THE ANGELS ... REGARD OUR SAFETY, UNDERTAKE
OUR DEFENSE, DIRECT OUR WAYS *and* EXERCISE A
CONSTANT SOLICITUDE THAT NO EVIL BEFALLS US.
John Calvin

Dear heavenly Father: Thank you for your powerful, majestic angels, who watch over me wherever I go. I'm comforted to know that you've assigned them to protect me. What an awesome gift. Amen.

Change of Heart

It's been in your thoughts so often this week that it's even made its way into your prayers—a picnic at the beach. Longtime friends. Favorite foods. Surf. Sand. Sun. But when the day finally arrives, storm clouds have gathered along with your faithful companions. As you set your blanket on a sandy knoll, the first drops of rain begin to fall. Before you can come up with plan B, the heavens seem to burst wide open, leaving your lunch as soggy as a sea sponge. As you and your friends run to your separate cars, you find yourself muttering under your breath, "So much for answered prayer."

If God is always listening, wholly loving and infinitely powerful, then why do some prayers seem to bounce off the walls of your room unanswered? The Bible talks a lot about prayer, but it doesn't unravel all of its mysteries. However, one thing it makes perfectly clear is that you're to talk to God about everything, anytime, anywhere. When you pray you invite God to become intimately involved in your daily life. You're not calling on a genie to make your fondest wishes come true; you're having a heart-to-heart chat with your heavenly Father. And like any loving parent, God will wisely answer your requests with "Yes," "No," or "Not yet."

God sees the big picture behind your prayers—consequences, opportunities, and obstacles that are beyond your understanding.

The more time you spend talking to him, the better you'll know and understand him. And the better you know him, the more your priorities will begin to resemble his. When you trust in his love for you, you'll be able to rest in his answer to your prayers, whatever they may be. You may find that some of your most treasured answered prayers aren't those that changed your circumstances but those that changed your heart.

Devote yourselves to prayer, being watchful and thankful.
Colossians 4:2

Delight yourself in the LORD
and he will give you the desires of your heart.
Psalm 37:4

ALL WHO CALL ON GOD IN TRUE FAITH, EARNESTLY
FROM THE HEART, WILL CERTAINLY BE HEARD *and* WILL
RECEIVE WHAT THEY HAVE ASKED AND DESIRED.
Martin Luther

Heavenly Father: Thank you for answering my prayers wisely as any loving parent would. Sometimes what I ask for and what I need are two different things. But you're never confused. You always know what's best for me. I receive your answers to each of my prayers with gratitude. Amen.

Dragon Slayer

IT TAKES COURAGE TO VENTURE out into uncharted water, no matter how calm, clear, or picturesque. As you look toward the distant horizon, your hand raised to shade your eyes from the glare of the afternoon sun, you picture what it would have been like to be an ancient explorer, to sail away from the only shore you've ever known, to believe that the world is flat and there's a chance your ship may sail right off the edge.

Although today there are few unexplored areas left in this world, other than the ocean floor itself, you still confront uncharted waters. You set sail every time you come face-to-face with the unknown—interacting with a stranger, waiting for a doctor's diagnosis, entering a new phase of parenthood, changing jobs, choosing to follow God's heart instead of your own. When what is unfamiliar lies dead ahead, you may be tempted to describe it the same way early mariners did: "Beyond this place there be dragons!"

Fear can turn anything into a dragon, if you let it. But with God you have the power to slay any dragons you encounter in this life. He is with you, guiding you, strengthening you, and encouraging you. He has the power to transform even your most difficult circumstances into something positive, something that will help you not only mature but thrive in the midst of trouble. Holding tightly to this truth is the key to living a courageous life.

Courage doesn't mean you'll never feel afraid. It simply means you're willing to risk moving forward, even when you're not entirely sure of what lies ahead. It means you're daily putting your trust in God to chart a safe course for you through rocky shoals so you can reach distant, unexplored shores, where buried treasure of eternal worth is sure to be found.

> *The LORD is my light and my salvation—*
> *whom shall I fear?*
> *The LORD is the stronghold of my life—*
> *of whom shall I be afraid?*
> Psalm 27:1

> *Have I not commanded you? Be strong and courageous.*
> *Do not be terrified; do not be discouraged, for the LORD*
> *your God will be with you wherever you go.*
> Joshua 1:9

COURAGE IS FEAR *that* HAS SAID ITS PRAYERS.
Dorothy Bernard

Dear Lord: I know you're always with me, but sometimes I see with my natural eyes and dismiss what my heart is saying. Thank you for your promise to go with me wherever I go. I will find courage in knowing you're right beside me every minute of every day, no matter what circumstances come my way. Amen.

That Sinking Feeling

THE RIPPLED WAVES ARE LAPPING against the side of the boat. You slip your jeans off from over your swimsuit, trade your tennies for a pair of swim fins, and ready yourself to dive into the azure water. That's when the guy next to you hangs his camera bag around your neck. Then he ties the laces of his heavy hiking boots together and slips them over your hand. Next, he unhooks the life vest you're wearing and pulls it on while placing his oversized leather motorcycle jacket over your tanned shoulders. Finally, he belly flops into the water unhindered as you stand there steaming in the sun—and it isn't just because the humidity is high. What are you going to do?

When it comes to relationships, it seems that some people would rather sink than swim. They allow what others have done to them—intentionally or unintentionally—to weigh them down. They willingly take on other people's baggage, carrying angry words, offenses, and grudges around like lead weights. But Jesus offers a better way to dive deep into the joys of life, swimming free and unencumbered, reaching out in relationship to others with a healed and healthy heart.

Forgiveness is the fishing knife that can free you from any relational net you've become tangled up in. It doesn't matter who's right or who's wrong. It doesn't matter whether the friend, stranger, or family member who has hurt you is sorry for what happened. What matters is that you're putting a stop to a self-destructive cycle

by freely offering others something God has offered you: forgiveness. Stop replaying those offenses in your mind. Pray for—instead of against—those who've offended you. Ask God to help you cut the net you're tangled in and let go of what's weighing you down so that you can hold on to him more tightly.

Forgive whatever grievances you may have against one another.
Forgive as the LORD forgave you.
Colossians 3:13

Peter came to Jesus and asked, "Lord, how many times shall I forgive
my brother when he sins against me? Up to seven times?"
Jesus answered, "I tell you, not seven times, but seventy-seven times."
Matthew 18:21–22

WHEN YOU FORGIVE, YOU IN NO WAY
CHANGE THE PAST—*but* YOU SURE DO
CHANGE THE FUTURE.
Bernard Meltzer

Dear Lord: It's just so hard to give up the right to be "right." So I hang
on to offenses that I should just let go. I harbor resentment and carry the
burden of unforgiveness until I'm stumbling under the load. Help me,
Lord, as I learn to let each offense slide off my back, forgiving so quickly
that the offense doesn't even have time to cling to me. Amen.

Freer Than the Sea

THE SEA HAS A FREEDOM that's easy to envy. The frothy brine can slip through the smallest crevice, fill vast undersea valleys, flow from one continent to another, move with the grace of a dolphin and the power of a freighter. Yet the freedom of the ocean is tempered by limits, the boundaries of a shoreline that cannot be crossed.

The freedom God offers is more limitless than a sea not bound by a shore. God's love, grace, and forgiveness free you from condemnation, guilt, and eternal separation from him. They enable you to grow and mature into the unique miracle God created you to be. They open the floodgates of your heart and mind so that joy, passion, and purpose can flow freely through your life. They enable you to put past mistakes behind you and walk boldly toward a new future with your head held high and your heart deemed pure.

This limitless freedom is a gift available to everyone. But not everyone truly wants to be free. Some people believe that saying yes to God will rob them of the freedom they have to do anything they please. It's true that following God may lead you in a different direction than you were once headed, but it's toward freedom, not away from it. You can trust that a God whose love for you is limitless only says no when what you want isn't what you need. Like putting a fifteen-mile-per-hour limit for speed boats near a shallow beach crowded with young families, the only limits God sets are those that will keep you, and those around you, safe. The more closely you follow him, the more freedom you'll discover you have to splash and play, learn and grow, laugh and love in the gentle wake of his tender care.

Now that you have been set free from sin and have become slaves to God, the benefit you reap leads to holiness, and the result is eternal life.
Romans 6:22

Jesus said, "If you hold to my teaching, you are really my disciples. Then you will know the truth, and the truth will set you free."
John 8:31-32

*F*REEDOM MEANS I HAVE BEEN SET FREE TO
BECOME ALL THAT GOD WANTS ME TO BE,
TO ACHIEVE ALL *that* GOD WANTS ME TO ACHIEVE,
TO ENJOY ALL THAT GOD WANTS ME TO ENJOY.
Warren W. Wiersbe

Dear Lord: It feels so good to be free, really free. I've never known anything like it. When I was following my own path, I thought I was free, but every day there was something new to weigh me down. I didn't feel good about myself or my actions. Thank you for removing all my burdens and replacing them with your wonderful gifts of love and grace. Amen.

A Familiar Shore

As you round the corner of the coastal highway, you catch sight of "your" beach, the one you return to year after year. You park the car where you always do, then make your way over the small series of dunes that point the way toward the rocky shore. Lugging your beach bag and picnic basket over to the spot of sand between the two rocks that remind you of dozing watchdogs, you carefully place your towel right where it belongs—beneath the windblown branches of your favorite tree. You sit quietly for a moment, drinking in every familiar detail, celebrating the fact that something in your life has remained the same.

There's comfort in the familiar. In knowing what to expect. In resting your weight on something you trust won't let you down. But the ground beneath your feet can shift. Over time rocks will erode from the caustic caress of the sun, salt, sand, and sea. One day even the tides will cease to draw the waves to and from the shore. Yet God's faithfulness to you will remain. More solid than a rock. More dependable than the ocean tides. More timeless than time itself!

God is the only true constant in this life and beyond. He doesn't say one thing and then do another. When he makes a promise, he keeps it. But don't confuse being faithful with being predictable. God's ways and words will often surprise you. That's when his faithfulness means the most. Even when your limited human understanding has a hard time wrapping itself around a limitless Lord, you can trust that what you know of his character—his love, mercy, grace, and strength—remains the same. Like your favorite beach, you can come to him again and again and find comfort, rest, and beauty in his familiar, steadfast presence.

> *Know therefore that the LORD your God is God; he is the faithful God, keeping his covenant of love to a thousand generations of those who love him and keep his commands.*
> Deuteronomy 7:9

> *The LORD is faithful to all his promises and loving toward all he has made.*
> Psalm 145:13

*I*N GOD'S FAITHFULNESS LIES ETERNAL SECURITY.
Corrie ten Boom

Heavenly Father: All my life I've longed for something or someone I could count on. Everyone in my life has let me down. Now I know that's what people do. They can't help it. They're only human. But you—you never let me down. You're always there to hear my prayers, to comfort me, to give me wisdom. I'm never alone. Thank you for your faithfulness. Amen.

Live Your Own Love Story

THE SIGHT OF A SHIP'S SAILS filled with a brisk sea breeze begins the opening credits of your own mental movie. As you watch the bow of the ship pitch and roll, you picture someone you love in the crow's nest, spyglass in hand, scanning the horizon, desperately searching the rocky shore for the treasure he's traveled across the wide and treacherous sea to find—you. With love as his compass, he's battled his way through storms, fought courageously against pirates, persevered on this hazardous journey when hope seemed as dim as the shadow of land on a distant horizon. There's nothing—not danger or suffering, disappointment or heartache, time or distance—that can keep him apart from the one he loves, or diminish the devotion he has for you.

But this love story isn't an idle fantasy. It's the real-life saga of Jesus' pursuit of you. He left a throne in heaven to walk the dusty roads of an often-hostile world to reach out to you in a way you'd understand. He pursued you through betrayal, suffering, and sacrifice. He was mocked, misunderstood, and ultimately left to die. But even death wasn't a distance far enough to keep him from you.

Jesus' love for you is deeper than the unexplored depths of the sea, truer than a navigator's compass, richer than any treasure this world has ever known. Nothing you've done can turn him away from you. The forgiveness he offers is as limitless as his love. All that's needed to make this love story complete is for you to love him in return.

Set sail on the adventure of a lifetime by opening your heart to the one who pursues you with an eternal passion. Jesus is near, extending his hand, inviting you to enter into a life with him that never ends, into a love you've always dreamed of.

As high as the heavens are above the earth,
so great is [God's] love for those who fear him.
Psalm 103:11

Nothing in all creation can separate us from God's love for us in
Christ Jesus our Lord!
Romans 8:39 CEV

JESUS DID NOT COME TO MAKE GOD'S LOVE POSSIBLE,
BUT *to* MAKE GOD'S LOVE VISIBLE.
Author Unknown

Dear Father: When I think about your love for me, I can't take it in. How could you love me? And yet you do! I know I'll never deserve your love, and that fills my heart even more with gratitude and thanksgiving. Lord, help me to love you more, to return some of the love you've poured out on me. Amen.

Through God's Eyes

THE WORLD'S TALLEST MOUNTAIN lies mostly beneath the sea. The highest point on Mauna Kea in Hawaii is only 13,796 feet above sea level, yet the mountain rises a total of 32,000 feet from the ocean floor. In contrast, Mount Everest, which is usually referred to as the world's tallest mountain, is only 29,035 feet tall. Everest rises higher above sea level than anything else on earth, making it appear to be the tallest mountain to those whose feet are planted on the ground. But not everything is as clear-cut as it seems.

Perspective can make a cruise ship look like a seagull on the horizon, or the world's tallest mountain appear to be an ordinary island peak. It can also make a friend appear to be an enemy, an opportunity look like a disaster, or your own abilities seem like liabilities rather than assets. Human perspective is always limited, not to mention often distorted.

The good news is that God's perspective isn't limited by your five senses, your emotional baggage, or even the constraints of time. God is omniscient, meaning that he knows everything. Only someone with all the facts can have a truly accurate perspective of any and every situation. And God has promised that if you ask him for the wisdom of his perspective, he'll gladly share it with you.

So when you're at a crossroads and unsure of which way to go, when troubles are brewing and you're not quite sure what lies beneath the surface, when you find yourself feeling as though what you do or who you are lacks value or purpose, take a moment to

gain a higher, truer perspective. Ask God to help you see your life through his eyes. Seeing things from God's eternal point of view can prevent you from making a mountain out of a molehill.

> *"My thoughts are not your thoughts,*
> *neither are your ways my ways,"*
> *declares the LORD.*
> *"As the heavens are higher than the earth,*
> *so are my ways higher than your ways*
> *and my thoughts than your thoughts."*
> Isaiah 55:8–9

> *How great are your works, O LORD, how profound your thoughts!*
> Psalm 92:5

WE SEE ACTUAL THINGS, AND WE SAY THAT WE SEE THEM,
but WE NEVER REALLY SEE THEM UNTIL WE SEE GOD;
WHEN WE SEE GOD, EVERYTHING BECOMES DIFFERENT.
Oswald Chambers

Dear Lord: So often I'm shortsighted, faithless, tied down by my own mis-perceptions. Raise my vision, I pray. Help me to sit on the high corner above the circumstances of my life and look down with eyes inspired by your eternal wisdom and understanding. I know that all you do is for my good. I believe that with all my heart. Amen.

Charting the Right Course

*L*OOKING OUT OVER THE WATER, you imagine you're adrift in the ocean, huddled in a lifeboat far from shore, with no known horizon in sight. You're alone, afraid, and uncertain of which way to even try to paddle your questionably seaworthy craft. But a flutter of hope compels you to lift your eyes from the soggy wooden slats beneath you to the heavens above. You scan the night sky for clues, sweeping the stars with your eyes as you might sweep a stray lock of hair from your forehead. There it is! The Big Dipper! Your eyes trace a path from the constellation straight to the North Star, Polaris—your compass point in the night. You dip your paddle into the salty sea, turning the small boat toward the steadfast star. The journey ahead may be difficult, but at least you know you're headed home.

You can feel lost at sea without finding yourself adrift in a literal lifeboat. Every day you're faced with countless choices, changing circumstances, complex relationships, and conflicting emotions. But you have a North Star that can help you find your bearings and guide you safely home. God's Word and his ways are more constant than Polaris. And their guiding light shines bright both day and night.

Don't drift aimlessly through another day. When you're unsure of which way to go, look up. Begin to plot your course of action by praying for wisdom. Read what the Bible has to say about the kinds of decisions you have before you. Ask others, whom you know God has led through similarly difficult times, to share with you what he has taught them along the way. Weigh their words and God's words, and the way you feel his Spirit leading you through prayer. Then put your paddle in the water, turn your lifeboat in the right direction, and row with all your might.

Trust in the LORD with all your heart and lean not on
your own understanding; in all your ways acknowledge him,
and he will make your paths straight.
Proverbs 3:5-6

If I rise on the wings of the dawn,
if I settle on the far side of the sea,
even there your hand will guide me,
your right hand will hold me fast.
Psalm 139:9-10

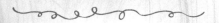

I KNOW NOT THE WAY GOD LEADS ME,
but WELL DO I KNOW MY GUIDE.
Martin Luther

Heavenly Father: I place my trust in you. Even when I feel lost and afraid,
unable to see even the very next step in front of me, I reach out for you and
you are there, as close as my breath. Thank you for leading and guiding me
each step along the way. You are truly an awesome God. Amen.

Temporary Treasure

THERE'S TREASURE BENEATH YOUR FEET. A glint of color. A swirl, a ripple, a curl of what looks like museum-quality porcelain. Like a shard of precious pottery, the fragile seashell beckons. It invites you to release it from the sand, hold it to your ear, run your fingers along its edges, ponder the life that once filled its now-empty form. You and the shell you hold have so very much in common.

Just like the sea creature who outgrew its temporary home, casting it off so it could better mature into the living work of art God designed it to be, you, too, will leave behind a shell one day. The time will come when your fragile frame will no longer be suitable for the person you're being transforming into—a permanent resident of heaven.

While there are more than fifty thousand different kinds of sea and snail shells known on earth, there are more than 6.5 billion unique human shells in use right now. Every minute, new shells are being formed as others are being left behind. Like the aquatic shells along the shore, these human shells are beautifully diverse, practical, breakable, and temporary.

But God has another "shell" waiting for you that will never be cast aside. When the day arrives for you to meet your Creator face-to-face, you'll be adorned with a body that will no longer age. Pain and tears will be a thing of the past. The earth and the heavens will be reborn as well, returned to their pre-Eden glory. The sun will no longer be needed because God's own brilliance will be heaven's light. That day you'll know the joy of being home at last.

But you're not there yet. Today, enjoy the temporary shell God has entrusted to your care. Just remember, although a shell is nice to look at, it's the life inside God values most.

If the earthly tent we live in is destroyed, we have a building from God, an eternal house in heaven, not built by human hands.
2 Corinthians 5:1

Never again will they hunger;
never again will they thirst.
The sun will not beat upon them,
nor any scorching heat.
For the Lamb at the center of the throne will be their shepherd;
he will lead them to springs of living water.
And God will wipe away every tear from their eyes.
Revelation 7:16–17

HEAVEN IS A PREPARED PLACE *for* A PREPARED PEOPLE.
Lewis Sperry Chafer

Dear Lord: What a wonderful promise you've given me—eternal life in a place where there will be no sadness or pain, only the joy of being in your presence. Remind me of this precious promise when times are difficult. It's simply a prelude to amazing things yet to come. Amen.

Child of the King

A SINGLE GRAIN OF SAND seems insignificant, especially in light of how many tons of sand cover shorelines around the globe—not to mention what lies beneath the waves. At first glance, one grain seems to bear an uncanny resemblance to any other. But if you stop along the shore, grasp a handful of sand, and then let a curtain of grains sift through your fingers back down to the ground, you'll notice that not every grain is the same. Some are darker in color. Others are more crystalline in appearance. Some resemble minuscule pebbles, while others are as fine as talcum powder. Subtle differences to be sure, but differences nonetheless. Just imagine what you'd see if you looked through a microscope.

People are much more complex, and diverse, than grains of sand. But in the hurry and scurry of modern life, it's easy to feel as though you're just as small, common, and inconsequential as a speck of sand on a crowded shore. But God wove you together in your mother's womb with loving intention. He has a purpose and a place for you in this world. He knows you more intimately than you know yourself. And he not only calls you by name; he calls you his child.

Although God's children are more numerous than the sand on the shore, every one is cherished as if he or she were an only child. So anytime your heart asks, "Who am I?" remind yourself of the fact that you're the beloved child of a sovereign King. Although you currently reside here on earth, your true home lies in heaven by his side. You don't have to wait until then to enjoy your royal ties and eternal relationship. The King is always at your side, an ever-attentive Father whose love is so strong that nothing, not even death, can separate you from him.

> *"Before I formed you in the womb I knew you,*
> *before you were born I set you apart," [says the Lord].*
> Jeremiah 1:5

> *Know that the LORD is God.*
> *It is he who made us, and we are his;*
> *we are his people, the sheep of his pasture.*
> Psalm 100:3

*H*E WHO COUNTS THE STARS AND CALLS
THEM BY THEIR NAMES IS *in* NO DANGER
OF FORGETTING HIS OWN CHILDREN.
Charles Spurgeon

Heavenly Father: Not only have you created me and redeemed me, but you have also made me your child, endowing me with all the privileges of life in a royal family. Thank you, dear Lord, for taking me as your own, when you could have more easily discarded your creation and started over. I owe all I have, and am, to you. Amen.

A New You

AT FIRST YOU WONDER if the oxygen from your dive tank is getting low. Maybe you're starting to hallucinate. What other explanation could there be for what's floating right in front of you, eyeing you as closely as you are it? Hidden in a shadowed reef, this sea creature appears to be mottled brown and black. Okay, calico. With whiskers that look like those of a freshwater catfish. It was the tail that first caught your attention, twitching back and forth like a metronome. But it's the fur, the webbed paws, and the quivering gills that have you doubting the fact that you actually rose from your bungalow by the sea and went for an early morning dive. Perhaps you're still in bed, having a nightmare about last night's fish dinner. It's either that or you've just discovered a new species, a totally new creation.

Although an aquatic cat sounds impossible, with God a totally new creation isn't impossible. As a matter of fact, new creations spring to life all the time. The instant you choose to put your life in God's hands, a miracle occurs. Your past mistakes are wiped away. Your future home in heaven is secure. And your heart begins to beat to a heavenly rhythm, one that moves you in God's direction.

So throw away your old preconceived notions about who you are and where you're headed in life. With God, your previous fears and weaknesses have lost their hold on you. What once seemed impossible is now within your reach. Grudges can be released. Wounds can be healed. Shame can be erased. And joy can begin to flow through your life in a constant tide that's no longer directed by circumstance. Take a good look at yourself through new eyes, courtesy of your heavenly Father. You'll discover a new creation, incalculably precious, uniquely gifted, a one-of-a-kind treasure chest of purpose and possibility.

If anyone is in Christ, he is a new creation;
the old has gone, the new has come!
2 Corinthians 5:17

In his great mercy [God] has given us new birth into a living
hope through the resurrection of Jesus Christ from the dead.
1 Peter 1:3

EACH DAY IS *a* NEW LIFE. SEIZE IT. LIVE IT.
David Guy Powers

Heavenly Father: Thank you for making me brand new—as holy and clean as the day I was born. I'm grateful first of all for the reprieve this new life gives me from guilt and shame. Then I thank you for the opportunity to live wisely, aware of my past mistakes but not destined to repeat them. Only the one who created me the first time could give me this gift of a second chance. Thank you. Amen.

Hunting for Truth

THE SUN IS BARELY PEEKING over the horizon. It's the perfect time for a solo swim. At least you thought you were solo. You do a double take. Maybe it's just a shadow. Another swimmer. A really big swimmer. Wearing gray trunks and grinning at you with a row of teeth that seem to go on forever. The theme from *Jaws* replays in your mind. You reprimand your runaway imagination. After all, you heard about the sightings. You heeded the warnings. You even chose to forgo your morning swim along the beach just to be on the safe side. So, instead you chose to take your morning dip in the hotel pool.

Sometimes the truth is hard to believe. But that doesn't make it any less true. If you're in a pool and notice that a shark has joined you for a few laps, the first thing you'll do is get out as quickly as possible—even if you can't come up with a logical explanation as to how the shark got there in the first place.

Not everything God says is easy to believe. But that doesn't mean it isn't true. God says that choosing to live your life outside of his care puts you in dangerous waters. You can spend your life arguing over things you don't understand, refusing to trust in someone you can't see. Or you can choose to put your faith in what you do understand: God is bigger than what you can see with your eyes and comprehend with your brain.

Reach out to God in simple faith. Hold tightly to the truth he's revealed to you so far. Act on what you already know. Trust him for what you don't. But don't hesitate to ask him for wisdom and understanding. He's promised that if you seek him and his truth, you're sure to find what you're looking for.

Jesus said, "If you hold to my teaching, you are really my disciples. Then you will know the truth, and the truth will set you free."
John 8:31-32

Jesus answered, "... For this I came into the world, to testify to the truth. Everyone on the side of truth listens to me."
John 18:37

No truths are simple, especially those of Scripture. But as we pursue them and participate in them more fully, *they* begin to reveal to us a life deeper and more integrated than we ever could have known otherwise.
Tim Hansel

Dear Lord: Forgive me when I fail to believe what you're clearly telling me, thinking somehow that what I see and hear and understand is all there is to truth. I know that there are unseen dangers in this world that are intent on my harm. I will listen carefully to your voice, Lord. Thank you for keeping me safe as I trust in your truth, even when I lack understanding. Amen.

Wise Ways

OCEANOGRAPHERS MAY KNOW lots of minutiae about the sea—how tide pools are formed, the chemical makeup of seawater, the geological stability of a specific underwater volcanic range, the biological differences between jellyfish and sea horses, or how many krill blue whales eat in a day. But if an oceanography team heads out into the Atlantic Ocean to study the habits of sea life during a storm, without preparing for the storm themselves, they haven't made good use of what they know. Team members may be smart, but they sure aren't wise.

Extreme example? Maybe not. Consider people who study the Bible. They know that God is faithful because they've read about how he came through for the Israelites at the Red Sea, how he rescued Daniel in the lion's den, and how he helped all his children in the book of Revelation. They've seen over and over throughout Scripture that God listens and responds to prayer. And they've learned that there are adverse consequences for choosing to ignore what he says. But what if these people continue to hold God at arm's length? What if they do whatever people around them are doing even when it goes against what God has said? What if they choose to worry instead of pray? Even if these people, smart people, can name every book in the Bible or recite verses from memory, in the end they'll be remembered as foolish instead of wise.

Walk in the ways of the wise. Put what you know into practice. What God is teaching you through the Bible and life itself isn't simply knowledge to be stored. It's wisdom to be lived out in every detail of your day. Ask God to guide you in how to best apply what you know. Then act on what you learn. It's not only a smart thing to do but a wise thing as well.

Wisdom is as good as an inheritance, an advantage to those who see the sun. For the protection of wisdom is like the protection of money, and the advantage of knowledge is that wisdom gives life to the one who possesses it.
Ecclesiastes 7:11–12 NRSV

Get wisdom, get understanding; do not forget my words or swerve from them. Do not forsake wisdom, and she will protect you; love her, and she will watch over you. Wisdom is supreme; therefore get wisdom. Though it cost all you have, get understanding.
Proverbs 4:5–7

OF ALL HUMAN PURSUITS, *the* PURSUIT OF WISDOM IS …
THE MOST PROFITABLE, THE MOST DELIGHTFUL.
Saint Thomas Aquinas

Dear Father: I've always considered myself to be a smart person. But I need to know how to apply that knowledge. Like Solomon in the Bible, I long to be wise. Thank you, Lord, for teaching me to be a wise steward of all the knowledge you've given me. Amen.

Sunday's Too Small to Hold It All

As THE MORNING LIGHT FILTERS down through the waves, the ocean floor resembles a vast pane of stained glass. Swirls of shadow and sunlight are pieced together with vivid accents of tangerine starfish and plum-colored sea urchins. Beds of kelp raise their hands in praise, swaying with the passing tides. A school of clown fish glides effortlessly through the silent sanctuary. They move as one body, first to the right and then to the left. Everywhere you look, you witness a living sermon giving testament to the God who created it all.

The worship the God of the universe deserves is too big and bold to be confined by the walls of a church building. Even though celebrating communion, singing praise songs, and bowing your head in corporate prayer with those who join you in calling your church "home" are all valid and wonderful ways of connecting with your heavenly Father, don't neglect the opportunity you have to turn every situation—including a day at the beach— into your very own worship service.

Don a snorkel mask instead of your Sunday best. Then venture into the saline sanctuary of the sea. Praise God for the wonder of all that's around you. Write your own saltwater psalm, allowing your thanks to float straight up to heaven's throne. Let the stillness of the underwater world help quiet your heart and mind. Listen for God's whisper in the gentle lapping of the waves against your mask. Bask in the joy of knowing you're wholly acceptable and deeply loved, even as you do nothing more than bob on the surface of the sea. Rest in the peace of this moment, this place, this single, rhythmic, life-giving breath. God is so big. Why shouldn't your gift of worship and praise become as boundless as the sea?

Ascribe to the LORD the glory due his name; bring an offering, and come before him. Worship the LORD in holy splendor; tremble before him, all the earth.
1 Chronicles 16:29–30 NRSV

I will give thanks to the LORD with my whole heart;
I will tell of all your wonderful deeds.
I will be glad and exult in you;
I will sing praise to your name, O Most High.
Psalm 9:1–2 NRSV

RECEIVE EVERY DAY AS A RESURRECTION FROM DEATH, AS A NEW ENJOYMENT *of* LIFE ... LET YOUR JOYFUL HEART PRAISE AND MAGNIFY SO GOOD AND GLORIOUS A CREATOR.
William Law

Dear Father: I do praise and worship you—for your love, your goodness, your forgiveness, your peace, your wisdom, your kindness, and for all the things you've done for me. I've never deserved any good thing from your hand, but you've blessed me despite my failings, and I thank you. Amen.

Invisible Transformation

MIND AND BODY AT REST, you lie still and serene in the sun. Fine white sand molds itself beneath your limbs, cradling you like a broad, endless hammock. The even rhythm of the waves has lulled you into a calm that feels timeless.

Drifting out of half sleep, you feel the sun's hot rays on your skin. A few more minutes—let them permeate just a little longer to make the cool water that much more refreshing.

Then you're up and awake, stepping into the surf and letting it splash over your skin. Rejuvenating! What an awesome day. The sun is just hot enough, and the temperature of the water is exactly right for cooling off.

You stand and peer down through the water all the way to the sandy, ridged surface at your feet, and you're struck by its unclouded appearance. You're aware that you're not alone in the miles of ocean surrounding you. You know that if you had microscopic vision, you'd be staring at hundreds of infinitesimally tiny creatures swimming around you. So how does the water stay so clean and clear?

The answer points to the genius of God, our wise and economic Creator. In the sea, nothing edible is wasted. The most microscopic bits are vacuumed up or filtered before they reach the ocean floor by tiny, busy creatures you and I will probably never view. They glean nourishment by eating what other plants and animals discard.

God, as it says in Romans 8, works everything together for

good. Nothing is wasted, and no detrimental thing is without another more hopeful aspect.

It can often be so hard to see clearly through the muck and confusion of painful circumstances in difficult times. How reassuring to have this hope: In every detail of life, the Lord is turning bad to good, using impossible situations for his glory.

This is a trustworthy saying that deserves full acceptance (and for this we labor and strive), that we have put our hope in the living God, who is the Savior of all men, and especially of those who believe.
1 Timothy 4:9–10

Let us hold unswervingly to the hope we profess, for [God] who promised is faithful.
Hebrews 10:23

I PLACE NO HOPE IN MY STRENGTH,
NOR IN MY WORKS:
but ALL MY CONFIDENCE IS IN GOD.
François Rabelais

Dear heavenly Father: Sometimes my circumstances are so big and my hope so small that I can barely see it. That's when I need you the most. As I look up into your bigness, your greatness, your power over the impossible, my hope grows strong again. That is, my hope in you and your love for me grows strong. And that's all the hope I need. Amen.

"HOLD THIS CONCH SHELL up to your ear. Can you hear the ocean?"

As a child, you found this fantastic suggestion is too intriguing not to put to the test, and too convincing not to fall for. You lifted the shell up and listened in fascination to the mysterious sounds emanating from its deep, vacant interior. Were you really listening to the roar of wind and waves? How could that be? Yet it had to be—just one of those unexplained wonders of nature!

How gullible you feel years later, when you smile to think how easily you were fooled.

It's a very convincing trick, though, and even as an adult, you can find it enchanting. Close your eyes and envision the crashing of breakers, the swirling of windswept sand. Analyze it scientifically, and you identify different kinds of waves—they're only sound waves bouncing around in there, producing sealike sound effects.

It's human nature to enjoy being harmlessly tricked now and then. But it's a trait that can leave you vulnerable to more dangerous forms of deceit. Evil quite often comes disguised, very convincingly, in palatable forms that appeal to you if you don't take the time to question or discern.

God has promised you wisdom, just for the asking. He wants to train you to discern good from evil, true from false. His Holy Spirit resides in you for this very purpose: so that you can be a bearer of integrity.

Integrity simply means that the outside matches the inside. Words fit with actions; intentions are pure and free from wrong motives. No false claims, no polishing up the exterior while hiding untruths and dark secrets within. God values authenticity in the believer because when you're free to be authentic, you're free to be fully his, inside and out.

Hold your life up to God's ear and let him hear the real you.

Search me, O God, and know my heart; test me and know
my anxious thoughts. See if there is any offensive
way in me, and lead me in the way everlasting.
Psalm 139:23–24

May integrity and uprightness protect me, because my hope is in [God].
Psalm 25:21

INTEGRITY IS *the* NOBLEST POSSESSION.
Latin Proverb

Dear Father: Keep me free from deceit, completely free. Don't allow me to
hedge at all. I give you permission to search my heart, minute by minute, and
reveal all that you find there that's not pleasing to you. I want, above all else, to
be a person of integrity in my words, my actions, and even my thoughts. Amen.

Beneath the Surface

It's quiet here on the sand. Except for the soft lapping of the waves on the shore, you hear nothing but the occasional seabird overhead. On the surface everything seems still and inactive. Yet a whole underground world houses a multitude of tiny creatures, working furiously at their jobs.

It's fascinating to consider the secret life of animals moving beneath the heavy weight of miles and miles of wet sand. Worms and other small burrowers work the earth and take nourishment from the nutrients that cling to the grains. Burrowing clams, shrimp, marine worms, and mole crabs—all designed to live and thrive, unseen and unheard, beneath the surface.

Much goes on beneath the surface in human beings as well. While smiles greet on the outside, hearts struggle on the inside. It's easy to have shallow exchanges and accept at face value that a friend is "fine, just fine." But you must listen closely to hear what's really there.

Jesus did this in his encounters with individuals. He listened, really listened, and always cut to the core of a person's real need.

The Samaritan woman at the well, unsure of how to hold a conversation with a Jewish man whom she expected would shun her completely, tried to talk about outward forms of religion, asking Jesus questions about how to worship and where to worship. But he drove straight to the point and confronted her about her unstable relationships, the symptoms of a hungry heart. He heard what wasn't being said (see John 4).

Jesus hears you, too. Not just what you reveal on the surface but the hidden person of the heart, your innermost being. He's never busy, distracted, or uninterested. He gives his full attention to you, revealing your heart's deepest secrets. He truly understands what you need and who you are. He's the God who really listens.

> You hear, O LORD, the desire of the afflicted;
> you encourage them, and you listen to their cry.
> Psalm 10:17

When you call upon me and come and pray to me, I will hear you. When you search for me, you will find me; if you seek me with all your heart.
Jeremiah 29:12–13 NRSV

THE FIRST DUTY *of* LOVE IS TO LISTEN.
Paul Tillich

Dear Father: Thank you for being a hearing God—the one who listens to my prayers and reads the secret intents of my heart. I know I need not mince words with you or throw hints. You know me well. You allow me to talk to you in my own way and my own time. You always receive me and hear me out. You listen, and then you answer me, speaking words of wisdom and courage to my hurting heart. Amen.

Ready for Anything

ONE FOOT ON THE SHORELINE of rock and sand, the other lightly caressed by shy, receding waters, you stand and survey what the tide has left behind.

Four times every day, the earth, sun, and moon do their complex dance of advance and retreat called the tides. In some parts of the world, this gravitational tug is powerful enough to strand ships and create havoc for coastal dwellers. In other places the level of movement is less dramatic.

What you're looking at now, a tide pool hollowed out to reveal plants and animals that were earlier submerged, is a remarkable result of this rhythm of the seas.

These plants and animals, in what is called the splash zone, are some of the most adaptable in God's creation. For one thing, they must be as comfortable on dry ground as they are in water. For another, they need to be able to survive in both sea water and the less predictable water of the tide pool—from very low salt in heavy rain to very high salt after hours of evaporation or low tide.

Contemplate the words of the apostle Paul: "I have learned to be content whatever the circumstances. I know what it is to be in need, and I know what it is to have plenty. I have learned the secret of being content in any and every situation…. I can do everything through him who gives me strength" (Phil. 4:11–13).

Just as every organism that dwells within the reach

of the tide must be able to survive in both water and air, your challenge as a Christian is to remain open to new experiences, both good and bad, that will test your faith and form your character.

And just as God has equipped his small sea creatures with the ability to adapt to their changing environment, he has given you all you need to thrive in your circumstances. Have faith in him, and you will be ready for anything!

I have learned to be content whatever the circumstances. I know what it is to be in need, and I know what it is to have plenty. I have learned the secret of being content in any and every situation, whether well fed or hungry, whether living in plenty or in want.
Philippians 4:11–12

I AM ALWAYS CONTENT WITH WHAT HAPPENS,
FOR I KNOW *that* WHAT GOD CHOOSES
IS BETTER THAN WHAT I CHOOSE.
Epictetus

Heavenly Father: Sometimes I think not wanting what I don't have is my greatest struggle. Still, I know that I'll never be at peace until I learn to be grateful for everything you give me and believe in my heart that what you give is all I really need. You're the God of enough. Help me to remember that each day and to trust you to be more than enough in my life. Amen.

Learning to Slow Down

YOU TAKE A DEEP BREATH of salty air and stretch, filling your lungs and then gradually letting them empty. What is it about the beach that so satisfyingly slows the pace of life? Time seems to linger here, refusing to be hurried. You have no choice but to match your inner rhythm to it, because it certainly isn't going to happen the other way around!

Patience is a lesson you can learn well from the sea. Think of the time it takes for wind and water to slowly erode proud and rugged rocks and smooth their jagged edges ... yet it happens, over the years, and these beautiful beaches of finely ground sand are the evidence.

Transformation of the shape of the shoreline itself is continual, yet it occurs imperceptibly, as each wave sweeps a few grains of sand along the shore or out to sea. And the change isn't usually imposed by sudden, crashing storm waves but by the regular parade of persistent, undulating waves.

The time it takes a pearl to be formed inside an oyster, the hours we wait as the earth turns slowly, steadily bringing light and settling into darkness at sunset—you live in a giant classroom, and patience is the daily lesson nature teaches us. Are you listening?

Those who study living things in the sea find that slow pace a recurring theme. Do you know that it takes an average sea star about three full hours just to find, open, and eat a four-inch abalone? Does away with the whole concept of fast food, doesn't it?

Spiritual growth also takes a patient heart. It doesn't happen over night but through continual submission to the cleansing, refining power of the Holy Spirit. Be patient. You're on your way to becoming all God created you to be. Hurrying just complicates the process.

You stoop to pick up a shell and wonder how long it's been rolled and polished by the surf. At first you think you might stash it away and take it back with you—an ocean souvenir. On second thought, you decide to toss it back, abandon it to its watery home. Let it slowly be rolled and polished until some of its roughness is worn away. It will only take a few decades. You can wait.

We want each of you to show this same diligence to the very end, in order to make your hope sure. We do not want you to become lazy, but to imitate those who through faith and patience inherit what has been promised.
Hebrews 6:11-12

If we hope for what we do not see, we wait for it with patience.
Romans 8:25 NRSV

TEACH US, O LORD, THE DISCIPLINES *of* PATIENCE,
FOR TO WAIT IS OFTEN HARDER THAN TO WORK.
Peter Marshall

Heavenly Father: I long to be the person you created me to be—flawless and polished, a fit vessel for your use. Give me the patience to keep working, learning, choosing rightly, believing that I'm fitting into your master plan by allowing you to wear away all my rough edges and draw out my eternal beauty. Amen.

Hold Fast to Jesus

YOUR BEACH EXPLORATION has brought you to a cozy cove
where light and shadows play, intermingled. Shallow pools gurgle
among smooth stones covered with lush beds of seaweed. Enjoying
the tickling-soft feel as it dances over your feet and slips between your
toes, you bend to examine this green, leathery plant with your fingers.

Its tender, downy touch is lovely, but what really strikes
you is its strength.

Because tide-pool plants are constantly exposed to opposing
elements—hours of sunlight and air exposure suddenly interrupted by
huge engulfing waves that last just as long—they thrive on hardship.

Algae lack roots, and instead grip on to their rock homes
with strong fibers called holdfasts.

Like relentless battering rams, the waves pound and pull,
thousands of times a day. But the holdfast remains true to its
name: It holds fast, utilizing the strongest glue that exists in
nature. In fact, it clings so tightly that the rock itself will break
before the algae is torn loose from it. And within its safety, many
little marine animals take refuge from the waves as well.

Jesus calls himself your Rock of Refuge, an unbreakable
stronghold. Your steadfast hope under life's toughest pressures
and the weight of its crushing blows, the Lord himself is your
anchor as well as your shelter. Staying close to him—abiding in
him—is your only hope for spiritual survival.

Seaweed exposed to the hot sun can blacken and become
brittle, but it won't usually dry out completely. When the tide

washes over it, it revives and becomes supple once more. This is because its stubborn fronds—its holdfasts—refuse to let go of the rock that ensures its life!

When hardships threaten to sweep you away, hold fast to Jesus and he'll enable you to persevere.

We are pressed on every side by troubles, but we are not crushed and broken. We are perplexed, but we don't give up and quit. We are hunted down, but God never abandons us. We get knocked down, but we get up again and keep going.
2 Corinthians 4:8–9 NLT

PERMANENCE, PERSEVERANCE, AND PERSISTENCE
IN SPITE OF ALL OBSTACLES, DISCOURAGEMENTS,
AND IMPOSSIBILITIES—IT IS THIS *that* IN ALL THINGS
DISTINGUISHES THE STRONG SOUL FROM THE WEAK.
Sir Francis Drake

Father: I intend to stand firm in my faith, never letting go of your hand. Yet I'm easily distracted, subject to wandering. Keep me close to you. Block my path should I begin to stray. Hold me close and never let me go. My safety, my salvation, my very life depend on you. Amen.

Responding to Change

A LAZY AFTERNOON FINDS YOU stretched out on the sand, at eye level with its glistening expanse of tiny crystal grains. You focus in on one pebble, lying so close that, in your mind's eye, it becomes a boulder. A slight breeze sends it tumbling a few inches. There goes a piece off Mount Everest, you muse.

In fact, that could very well be possible!

Sand is nothing more than crushed rock, and the millions of granules you see around you have traveled miles, from every part of the planet.

Sand is always in motion. Although a broad, level beach may appear still and stable, in truth, the motion of tides, currents, and spinning gusts of air incessantly rearrange it.

From season to season, great changes can occur in the landscape by the breaking waves' redistribution of sediment, and sandbars can move many feet to create or wipe out a whole series of dunes.

Isn't it amazing to think that God oversees all of this action, that the motion of not a single grain escapes his notice?

As in nature, change is the predominant force in God's master plan for the seasons of your life. What may seem a random incident—some small surprise or major disappointment that interferes to shift your present course—is merely a piece of the puzzle that is constantly arranging itself beneath his sovereign hand.

Your response to change says a lot about your faith in God's plans for you. Do you believe that God allows the events and circumstances you encounter in life for your good? Do you look for his hand in the changes, or do you doubt his presence and wonder if he really cares? Do you trust him or give in to fear?

You are so much more precious to God than the shifting grains of sand. He values you far above other created things. Bend with his changes, go where he sends you, and believe that your loving God has good plans for you.

"I know the plans I have for you," declares the LORD, *"plans to prosper you and not to harm you, plans to give you hope and a future."*
Jeremiah 29:11

The plans of the LORD *stand firm forever,*
the purposes of his heart through all generations.
Psalm 33:11

NEVER BE AFRAID TO TRUST AN
UNKNOWN FUTURE *to* A KNOWN GOD.
Corrie ten Boom

Father God: How good you are to me. Not only do you pull me out of the destruction I have reaped by my own devices, but you reinstate purpose and meaning through your plans for my life—plans you developed before the foundation of the earth, plans that no one can deter. Thank you, Lord, for unfolding your plan before me as I lay my life at your feet. Amen.

Letting Go... of Whatever It Takes!

SYMMETRY. HOW PLEASING IT IS TO THE EYE. Spending time near the ocean has deepened your appreciation for both simple and complex marine life, and you've noticed how much beauty is often due to symmetry in design.

That's why it's disturbing, on some level, to spot a creature with a missing limb. It's odd to see a crab, a shrimp, or a lobster scuttling along with one less leg or claw than it should have. It's especially disconcerting to discover a sea star with one vanished or stunted ray. You wonder, Will it grow back?

It won't grow back if it was severed as a result of some accident or injury, but if it was shed naturally, by what is known as autotomy, nature will replace it in time.

What happens with autotomy is this: To elude a predator, the escaping creature simply drops its captured limb and takes off. God has equipped certain animals with this ability, and from it you can learn to escape the clutches of sin.

When Potiphar's wife tried to seduce Joseph, he didn't stick around to flirt with temptation. He left her clutching his cloak and ran for all he was worth (Gen. 39:4–20).

At some point in your walk with God, you may feel reluctant to give up something he wants you to leave behind for your own good. You may wonder what your life will look like without it, yet in your heart you know it's a source of stumbling and could easily harm you.

Don't hesitate to surrender yourself to the Lord. In his pruning process, he has your ultimate good in mind and wants to free you of anything that could rob you of his best for your life. If he asks you to surrender a part of yourself, know that his goal is to restore you, in his time, to divine balance.

Submit yourselves, then, to God. Resist the devil,
and he will flee from you.
James 4:7

Let us throw off everything that hinders and the sin that so easily
entangles, and let us run with perseverance the race marked out for us.
Hebrews 12:1

I HAVE HELD MANY THINGS IN MY HANDS,
AND I HAVE LOST THEM ALL; *but* WHATEVER I HAVE
PLACED IN GOD'S HANDS, THAT I STILL POSSESS.
Corrie ten Boom

Lord God: I want to be pure and clean in your presence. Help me as I sur-
render my all to you—my words, actions, thoughts, desires, secrets, hopes.
Sustain me, Lord, as I surrender my pride, ambition, and fears. I give
you my heart and soul and body. I'm not afraid, for I know that you can
be trusted. Amen.

Enjoying the View

YOU'VE DRIVEN MANY MILES to savor this ocean view for a few brief days. Now your vacation has come to an end and you reluctantly head home. The evening sun is setting, and permanent beachfront residents are turning on their lights. Through their windows you see ordinary people going about their ordinary business.

You think to yourself, What I wouldn't give to be here all year long! I wonder if they know how lucky they are.

It's a strange thing about human nature, though—how easily we take things for granted. What seems like an unattainable dream for one person—whose desires are also, frustratingly, just out of reach—is a ho-hum reality for another.

The children of Israel, while slaves in Egypt, wanted nothing more than their freedom. But once Moses led them out of that country, instead of rejoicing in their liberty—and the nearness of the Promised Land—they complained about the manna God had given them to eat, moaning and mourning the loss of the goodies they remembered having in captivity (see Num. 11).

How easy it is for us to idealize living full time on the beach. Or in the mountains. Or anywhere but where life has happened to land us.

A grateful heart brings joy in any circumstance. Wherever you are, try seeing your surroundings with new eyes. Imagine that the vista outside your window is what a passing motorist envies;

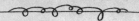

your situation in life that appeals to someone less fortunate. Because, no doubt, that's the case.

Your quiet, settled heart speaks louder to those who don't know the Lord than any well-chosen words. Look to God and be thankful. Enjoy the view, right where you are!

Just as you received Christ Jesus as Lord, continue to live in him, rooted and built up in him, strengthened in the faith as you were taught, and overflowing with thankfulness.
Colossians 2:6–7

Let them give thanks to the LORD for his unfailing love and his wonderful deeds for men, for he satisfies the thirsty and fills the hungry with good things.
Psalm 107:8–9

CULTIVATE THE THANKFUL SPIRIT!
IT WILL BE *to* YOU A PERPETUAL FEAST.
John R. MacDuff

Father God: Should I live to be a thousand years old, I could never begin to thank you for all you've given me. You owed me nothing, and yet you've given me everything I have. I'm thankful for your kindness, your generosity, your goodness. You are indeed a mighty God and a tender, thoughtful provider. Amen.

Real Achievement

"THE LOGIC OF WORLDLY SUCCESS rests on fallacy," said writer Thomas Merton, "the strange error that our perfection depends on the thoughts and opinions and applause of other men."

Against the immensity of the ocean, personal successes and achievements back home seem small and inconsequential. That's because real achievement—the kind that isn't based on what others say about you—depends on something much more important; namely, the kind of person you are.

Look out over the vast body of water before you. Awesome! But if you knew it to be only ankle deep as far as your eyes can see, you probably wouldn't think it so marvelous. You're in awe because you know that the ocean is more than surface ripples, even more than towering waves. It possesses depth—great depth.

Real achievement requires depth of character, for without it achievements evaporate, leaving nothing but a shallow pond. Look at that water again. It houses all sorts of living things—fish, plants, and other organisms. Real achievement, too, embraces life. It strives for excellence. It nurtures and promotes the achievements and successes of others. It accepts scorn or applause, indifference or excitement with equanimity, just as the surface of the sea reflects both clouds and sunshine. And real achievement—no matter what the thoughts and opinions of others, or the lack or presence of their applause—never ends. The tides ebb and flow, yet the depths of the ocean remain calm. Real achievement is the ability to continue being true to yourself in all circumstances.

God, Creator of all, always looks beneath the surface. He knows what Jesus Christ has achieved in your life, and he sees you as his beloved child. You possess the power of his Spirit to achieve all things he has in mind for you. And even if the whole world applauds you, it means nothing, because the Lord himself says, "Know what? You're awesome!"

Whatever your task, put yourselves into it, as done for the Lord and not for your masters, since you know that from the Lord you will receive the inheritance as your reward; you serve the Lord Christ.
Colossians 3:23–24 NRSV

Commit your work to the LORD, and your plans will be established.
Proverbs 16:3 NRSV

THE ROOTS OF TRUE ACHIEVEMENT LIE IN THE WILL TO BECOME THE BEST *that* YOU CAN BECOME.
Harold Taylor

Heavenly Father: I lay my achievements at your feet, for I know that my strength, my motivation, my perseverance come from you. Without you, I could achieve nothing. Thank you for keeping my head on straight, for helping me to see amid all the applause that you are the one who brings me success. Amen.

At One with God

As you spend time strolling along the shore or sitting on the beach, breathe the fresh air and relax. You're away from all the distractions of busy days back home. Set your mind at rest and really listen to and observe the earth, sea, and sky.

You may be using this time of physical and emotional renewal for spiritual refreshment as well. Looking deep within your soul as you contemplate almighty God, you see him on his throne, perfect, mighty, and holy. Then a distraction: the pinch of sin. The weight of guilt. These things come between you and God, as surely as a tall brick wall built on the shore would come between you and the glorious vista before you. Human imperfection, weakness, and transgression hide God's love, blur his mercy, and often conspire to persuade people that no relationship with him is possible—or that it's attainable only through human effort.

Jesus Christ, God's beloved Son, came to atone for the sins of the world—to make it possible for you have a relationship with almighty God. To do this, Jesus took on himself the guilt of human sin and endured God's punishment through his suffering and death on Calvary. God raised him from the grave to prove that he had torn down the great barrier standing between the human and the divine, making available to all who come to him the cleansing tide of his righteousness. His atonement washes away anything that would block your relationship with him.

As you contemplate the deep waters, remind yourself of

God's deep love for you—the love that guarantees your allegiance with him now and through eternity. Scan the horizon and remember he has removed your transgression from you "as far as the east is from the west" (Ps. 103:12). The next time the tide cleanses the shore, give thanks for the righteousness that is yours through Jesus Christ. Rest in the serenity of nature—at peace with God.

This is love: not that we loved God, but that he loved us and sent his Son as an atoning sacrifice for our sins.
1 John 4:10

[Jesus Christ] is the atoning sacrifice for our sins, and not only for ours but also for the sins of the whole world.
1 John 2:2

When we are filled with the Holy Spirit, he unites us body, soul, and spirit with God until we are one *with* God even as Jesus was. This is the meaning of the Atonement— at-one-ment with God.
Oswald Chambers

Dear Father: What an honor it is to know that because you reached out to me through Jesus, I can be one with you—one in purpose, one in thought, one in action. Thank you for giving your very own Son to atone for my sins and offer me another chance at life. Amen.

Clap Your Hands

IT'S A SUNNY DAY at the seashore—you can't help but smile! You're listening to the sound of the surf, not the say-so of the boss. (You did leave your cell phone in the hotel room, didn't you?) You're wearing nothing except a swimsuit and a layer of sunscreen, and nothing on your feet except sand. As the kids' song says, "If you're happy and you know it, clap your hands!"

As a Christian, you have more reasons than being on a beach vacation to be happy. First, you know where you are. Is it possible that everything around you—miles of coastal rock formations and cliffs for climbing, acres of seashells for collecting, a vast expanse of water for fishing, swimming, and surfing—took shape by happenstance? Not a chance! You're relaxing in a warm and sunny corner of God's glorious creation. Second, you know who you are. Just one person among many sunbathing on the sand? No. You're a beloved child of God. Third, you know whose you are. The world's? Never! You know you belong to Christ, who calls you his sister, his brother. Fourth, you know how you feel about all this. Anxious? Angry? Resentful? Of course not. More like thankful. Joyous. Happy. You know who rules the marvels and mysteries of creation and who has given you the gift of rest and relaxation, and you don't need to ask why. It's because of love—God's love for you.

If you came here for an attitude adjustment, you came to the right place. Clap your hands right now—you're on vacation and you're at the beach. But what if it's raining? What if everything isn't absolutely perfect? Go ahead and try out your hand-clapping-happy attitude anyway. When you know you belong to God, you might just want to clap your hands every day of your life, come rain or shine!

You have made known to me the path of life;
you will fill me with joy in your presence,
with eternal pleasures at your right hand.
Psalm 16:11

This is the day the LORD has made;
let us rejoice and be glad in it.
Psalm 118:24

CIRCUMSTANCES AND SITUATIONS DO COLOR LIFE,
BUT YOU HAVE BEEN GIVEN *the* MIND TO CHOOSE
WHAT THE COLOR SHALL BE.
John Homer Miller

Awesome Father: Thank you for this vacation—time to kick back and relax in the abundance of your love and peace. Show me those little things that I too often overlook when I'm back home focused on work and responsibility. Then show me how to take a happy, grateful attitude back with me when I return home. Receive my thankfulness. Amen.

An Open Book

YOU SPEND A LOT OF TIME looking out over the ocean. You appreciate its hues at different times of the day, how the sun spreads a golden path on the water's surface, how the sky seems to melt into the horizon at dawn and dusk. You think about the relationship of moon and tides, sand and water, sky and sea. Yes, there's a Creator. But if you stop there, you know only half the story.

In the Bible, God tells you the rest of the story. He identifies himself as the one who created the earth, sea, and sky, and everything else that exists. He even says how he did it: He spoke it into being. Then he talks about relationships—his to you, yours to him. He says that he knew you before you were born and loved you then as much as he loves you now. In a perfect world—the way he created it—you would be able to return his love naturally and effortlessly. But it's not a perfect world, and the Bible tells you how it became imperfect. The Bible details the bad news of sin only to celebrate the good news of salvation through Jesus Christ, who shines on you with grace, mercy, and peace. Yet even now you haven't heard the whole story! The Bible goes on to reveal God's many promises to you ... his promise to stay with you, to help you, to strengthen you. His promise to love you, to care for you and about you, to nurture the relationship he started with you before time began.

Go ahead and soak in the sights, sounds, tastes, and textures all around you. Then tell the one who created it all how much you appreciate his work. You know him because he has told you the whole story in his book, the Bible.

The man who looks intently into the perfect law that gives freedom,
and continues to do this, not forgetting what he has heard,
but doing it—he will be blessed in what he does.
James 4:25

Everything that was written in the past was written to teach us,
so that through endurance and the encouragement of
the Scriptures we might have hope.
Romans 15:4

THE BIBLE IS A LETTER FROM GOD
with YOUR PERSONAL ADDRESS ON IT.
Søren Kierkegaard

Great Father: My eyes can barely take in the magnificence around me, and yet this is but a small part of all you've created. Thank you for giving me the Bible so that I can understand why you did all you did and what you expect from me. It brings peace and security to my life and my relationship with you. Amen.

Everyday Blessings

As YOU STROLL ALONG the beach, you savor the vast, majestic scene before you. That's understandable! But today as you walk, look down at the sand. There you find a carpet of tiny shells and pebbles at your feet. You bend down to pick up a handful of shells, each of them a masterpiece of design, texture, and hues. Pebbles, polished by the surf, feel smooth and cool in your hand. The sea gives all these small treasures in abundance. They're available to anyone who comes along, who's willing to stop, bend down, pick them up, and look at them.

You can easily name the big, ocean-sized blessings in your life. They're the obvious things like health, family, friends, work, food, shelter—and life itself. But it takes willingness to pause and look to discover the myriad little treasures God puts in your path. They're the simple blessings, the delightful things he makes available to you in abundance each day. And all for free. A light heart. A peal of laughter. A kindly smile. A thoughtful word, an engaging book, a funny movie. A child's hand in yours. A full moon over the ocean. Giraffe-shaped clouds floating overhead. A googly eyed frog in a pond. The rhythmic rush of the waves, the rustling whisper of wind through the trees.

While you're at the beach, why not find a few exquisite shells and smooth pebbles to put in your pocket. Touch them frequently to remind yourself of the abundance of tiny treasures God puts all around you—even on the ground you walk on. Then back home, lay your treasures in a spot where you'll see them each day.

Let them remind you that no matter where you are, God showers you with blessings, both ocean-big and seashell-small. For all his blessings, give him thanks and praise.

From the fullness of [Jesus'] grace we have all
received one blessing after another.
John 1:16

How great is your goodness, which you have stored up for those who
fear you, which you bestow in the sight of men
on those who take refuge in you.
Psalm 31:19

LIFT UP YOUR EYES.
THE HEAVENLY FATHER WAITS TO BLESS YOU—
IN INCONCEIVABLE WAYS *to* MAKE YOUR LIFE
WHAT YOU NEVER DREAMED IT COULD BE.
Anne Ortlund

Dear Lord: You've overwhelmed me with your generosity. Your blessings
follow me everywhere I go. Even when I pass through a dark valley, I have
the blessing of your presence with me. Thank you for every gift you've
given me—big and small. You're a wonderful, giving God. Amen.

A Firm Anchor

You've spent a good part of each day at the beach looking out over the ocean, and you haven't seen the same color combination twice. From deep blue to steel gray, from light turquoise to sun-kissed gold, the ocean's moods change with the hours, days, and seasons. You see, too, how the movement of the water can change quickly and unexpectedly. You watch in wonder as the ocean rises and falls with great force in the throes of a violent story, and you ponder the mystery of its great expanse shrouded by the darkness of a moonless night. Then in the middle of a perfect summer's day, you bask in the serenity of its cool and gentle waters.

The ocean and all things this side of heaven change. Without a doubt, you've experienced plenty of change in your life, some of it welcome and some of it heartbreaking. Birth and rebirth, newness and renewal, make your life shimmer the way water shines when illuminated by bands of sunshine. Times of waiting, regret, and endings cast long shadows, and times of darkness compel the troubled soul to seek the light of God's comfort, wisdom, and guidance. Times of turmoil and destruction—when storms of change toss you into uncharted seas—give way to times of serenity and peace—when you rest and refresh yourself in the calm waters of God's enduring care.

Perhaps you've come to the beach seeking solace, a brief refuge from a difficult and saddening change in your life. Look to the ocean today and tomorrow and the next day. Let its colors, its texture, its moods remind you that change is nature's way of bringing about new beginnings. It's God's way of leading you to newness of life. And though all things change, God never changes. He continues to be your guiding light in every darkness. He remains your firm anchor through all the changing seas of life.

Jesus Christ is the same yesterday, and today and forever.
Hebrews 13:8

Every good and perfect gift is from above, coming down from the Father of the heavenly lights, who does not change like shifting shadows.
James 4:17

THERE STANDS, BEHIND ALL THAT CHANGES
AND CAN CHANGE, *only* ONE UNCHANGEABLE JOY....
THAT IS GOD.
Hannah Whitall Smith

Great changeless God: I take comfort in the fact that even when the world around me is changing at lightning speed, you don't change. You stay the same, completely steady, even as the universe swirls before you. I know I can count on you, that you'll deal fairly with me each and every time. Your laws won't change, and neither will your love for me. You're my refuge in the storm, and I thank you. Amen.

BEACH PRAYERS • 77

Gentle Currents

RIP CURRENTS—STRONG CURRENTS FLOW-
ING from shore out to sea—cause hundreds of
drowning every year. Lured by the sight of apparently calm
waters, bathers wade in and then suddenly find themselves
gripped by a powerful channel of water that pulls them out
to sea. Panicked, some victims make the wrong choice.
They try to swim against the current—back to shore—but
they soon exhaust themselves in their futile effort. To
swim out of a riptide, you must swim parallel to the shore
until you've left the current's channel.

Unlike an undertow, rip currents work at the surface. Unusually calm water with shore-to-sea ribbons of
brownish foamy water indicate rips, and they can be present wherever there are breaking waves, including in large
lakes. Although rips form any time of day, they're preva-
lent at low tide. Warning flags on lifeguard stations or
signs posted along the shore need to be taken seriously.

This vacation comes as a welcome getaway. In the
days before you left home, you felt a bit overwhelmed,
pulled by the often conflicting currents of duty, responsibility, and the expectations of others.

Like rip currents, a crowded calendar can pull you
where you don't want to go. Also like rips, there are signs:
no white space in your daily planner, stress-related health
issues, lack of pleasure in your daily activities, the feeling

of being out of control. When this happens, you need to make choices. The wrong choice would have you swimming against the facts—denying there's a problem or forcing yourself to do it all, regardless of the consequences. The right choice calls for you to swim alongside your calendar and assess your days. Ask God to guide you in letting go of some things and in doing other things better. With him, choose to swim out of calendar rips and into the gentle currents of a fulfilling and joyful life.

This is what the LORD says: "Stand at the crossroads and look; ask for the ancient paths, ask where the good way is, and walk in it, and you will find rest for your souls."
Jeremiah 6:16

THERE IS A TIME WHEN WE MUST FIRMLY CHOOSE THE COURSE WE WILL FOLLOW, *or* THE RELENTLESS DRIFT OF EVENTS WILL MAKE THE DECISION.
Herbert V. Prochnow

Dear Lord: Help me to deal wisely with the affairs of my life, handling rip currents with courage and intelligence. When I find myself fighting to stay afloat, I'll remind myself to relax and let you pull me along until the danger has passed. Thank you for being my rescuer of first resort. Thank you for your patient, loving care. Amen.

A Great Beginning

LONG BEFORE SEA TRAVEL, coastal people felt the pull of the great waters. In lyrical song and epic poem, they imagined what might lie beyond the horizon. They imagined all sorts of things—paradise, nothingness, exotic lands, never-ending seas. But they really didn't know what was there because no one who had ventured out had ever come back.

God, who created the world and still preserves it, has promised that he will return. The Bible is clear on the subject. At a particular time in history—known only to God—Jesus will return in glory. Everyone in the world will see him. No debate about whether or not "this is it." No doubt as to his identity. Surely, some people shudder at the prospect, but not his people. God's people will welcome him as the one who ascended into heaven on the clouds and has now returned the same way.

As one of God's own, you know him as your Father, your Savior and Redeemer, your Comforter. He calls you by name and has put you on this earth to enjoy its beauty and its blessings. Because he has told you in his Word, you know that his return means the beginning of your eternal life with him and all the saints. If you think the ocean is majestic, just wait until you see heaven! There will be glory and splendor beyond words.

If Christ were to return right now, what kind of welcome would you give him? Open arms, a joyful shout, and a heart filled with gratitude for the majesty of his creation spread out before you would be a great beginning to your eternal life in him!

[Jesus said,] "In my Father's house are many rooms; if it were not so, I would have told you. I am going there to prepare a place for you. And if I go and prepare a place for you, I will come back and take you to be with me that you also may be where I am."
John 14:2–3

In keeping with [God's] promise we are looking forward to a new heaven and a new earth, the home of righteousness.
2 Peter 3:13

WE ARE NOT A POST-WAR GENERATION; *but* A PRE-PEACE GENERATION. JESUS IS COMING.
Corrie ten Boom

Dear Father: I try to imagine what it will be like when you come again. What will it be like to see you face-to-face? I know it will be wonderful. Show me how to properly prepare for that day. I want to be pleasing in your sight when you come. Amen.

Feeding Time

TIDAL POOLS FORM ALONG ROCKY coastlines when high tide fills depressions on the beach. A tidal pool nurtures crabs, starfish, mussels, snails, whelks, and sea anemones, as well as other marine animals and plants. The ocean's daily tides replenish and circulate water through the sheltered pool, and sunlight reaches the floor of the pool to sustain its inhabitants. If tides fall short and the sun dries the pool, life within the pool dies.

In a similar way, Christian growth dies if it isn't watered faithfully and regularly. The faith life of a Christian who doesn't spend time each day in God's Word sooner or later dries up. The rate and vibrancy of your Christian growth depends on the work of God's Spirit in you, and his Spirit works in you through his Word. Without the constant replenishment of his guidance, his promises, and his comfort in your heart and mind, you subject the life-giving waters of your faith to the scorching temperatures of temptation, and heat has a way of evaporating pools of water.

To grow, your faith requires time set aside for you to focus on God alone. Time to actively praise him, fervently pray to him, mindfully study his Word, and quietly meditate on its meaning for your life. As a tide pool depends on daily tides to supply it with fresh nutrients, so your growth in Christ depends on a constant stream of his sacred food. As a growing Christian, you also need to open yourself to the sunlight of self-examination. Good spiritual health harbors no secret crevices or dark shadows. A growing faith life thrives on your eagerness to immerse yourself in God's Word so you can meet the harsh environment of a sin-parched world with the cool waters of wisdom, truth, and love.

Jesus said to them, … "Others, like seen sown on good soil, bear the word, accept it, and produce a crop—thirty, sixty or even a hundred times what was sown."

Mark 4:20

Cultivate these things. Immerse yourself in them. The people will all see you mature right before their eyes! Keep a firm grasp on both your character and your teaching. Don't be diverted. Just keep at it.

1 Timothy 4:15–16 MSG

CHRISTIAN SPIRITUALITY DOES NOT BEGIN WITH US TALKING *about* OUR EXPERIENCE; IT BEGINS WITH LISTENING TO GOD CALL US, HEAL US, FORGIVE US.

Eugene H. Peterson

Dear Lord: More than anything, I want to grow in my relationship with you. Help me as I strive to eat the spiritual food—prayer and the study of your Word—that will make me strong and faithful in my walk with you. I willingly lay my life before you so you can search me and expose anything offensive to you. Thank you, Lord, for the privilege of knowing you better each day. Amen.

Rest and Relaxation

THE RHYTHMIC RUSH OF THE WAVES
sweeps worries aside. The distant horizon puts the
small irritations of life in perspective. The simple majesty of the
ocean soothes and comforts a tired mind and body. For relaxation
and stress relief, you've come to the right place. But when your
soul cries out for rest, there's a better place to be.

Jesus invites all weary souls to come to him. He offers rest
and a release from the afflictions that weigh you down. How does
he do it? First, he says simply, "Give that load to me." He relieves
you from the burden of believing that you need to handle everything yourself.

Second, he invites you to learn from him. In his Word, he
shows you by his own example that he has compassion on people.
He healed the sick, fed the hungry, and forgave the sins of all. He
proclaimed the Father's unchangeable and eternal love, then proved
it by accepting death on the cross to win sinful people his perfect
righteousness. Knowing he cares so much about you, you can rest
assured that he's going to care about the concerns you bring to him.

And third, he changes your perspective. Once your load is
removed from your shoulders and your trust placed in his care,
you see something you couldn't see before: the long view. The
heavenly view. God's promise of eternal life cuts this life and all
its problems down to size. You know this isn't all there is any
more than a pail of saltwater is all there is of the sea.

The beach is the right place to come for your much-needed and well-deserved rest and relaxation. When it's your spirit needing R & R, however, come to Jesus—the best place of all.

The LORD is my shepherd, I shall not want.
He makes me lie down in green pastures;
he leads me beside still waters;
he restores my soul.
He leads me in right paths for his name's sake.
Psalm 23:1–3 NRSV

[Jesus said,] "Are you tired? Worn out? ... Come to me. Get away with
me and you'll recover your life. I'll show you how to take a real rest."
Matthew 11:28 MSG

IN CHRIST THE HEART OF THE FATHER IS REVEALED, THE
HIGHER COMFORT THERE CANNOT BE *than* TO REST IN THE
FATHER'S BOSOM.
Andrew Murray

Dear Lord: I surrender myself to you. Tired, discouraged, alone, help me
to rest in your love and slowly lay all my burdens at your feet. Teach me
how to hear your voice daily rather than waiting until I can barely lift my
head. And show me how to live with eternity in mind. Amen.

Son Shine

SUNLIGHT BATHES THE OCEAN'S SURFACE in shimmering patterns of blue, green, and gold. Dappled waves of water mirror the sun's path across the sky from dawn to dusk. Even on a cloudy day when the sun's reflection dims to shades of gray, the sun continues to shine above the clouds.

Christ has committed himself to you just as God committed the sun to the water below it. On clear days the water reflects the sun with no hindrance. From shore to horizon, it's so bright you need to put on your sunglasses. Ideally, every Christian would reflect God so brilliantly that people would grab for their glasses, but in fact that's rarely the case. On this side of heaven, things come between you and the Son. Clouds of temptation hover over you, attempting to cast on you their shadows of guilt and blame. Storm clouds gather on the horizon, threatening to blot out the Son and cast you into a turbulence of doubt and darkness. Look out over the water, however, and remind yourself that the sun—and the Son—can disperse the thickest of clouds. Then notice how currents of water move and bend the sun's rays. Similarly, human reasoning, popular opinion, and overwhelming emotions often bend and distort the pure light of God's love. Some people find it hard to believe that God would continue—or even start—to shine his love down on them, but he does. He's made a commitment, and he keeps his commitments.

God is as committed to you as the sun to the ocean. Though clouds drift between you, though various currents pull you this way and that, though your commitment to him falters from time to time, he's always there for you. He's ready and willing to banish the clouds, calm the waters, and shine his glorious light on you.

I will establish my covenant as an everlasting covenant between me and you and your descendants after you for the generations to come, to be your God and the God of your descendants after you.
Genesis 17:7

He is the LORD our God; his judgments are in all the earth. He remembers his covenant forever, the word he commanded, for a thousand generations, the covenant he made with Abraham, the oath he swore to Isaac.
Psalm 105:7–9

GOD'S GRIP IS SUPERNATURALLY TIGHT. ONCE YOU HAVE GIVEN YOURSELF TO HIM, HE WILL NEVER LET YOU GO.
Andrea Garney

Dear Father: I can't imagine why you would commit yourself to me, as well as all your resources to meet my needs. But you do! Such knowledge amazes and thrills me. Though I can't comprehend it, I receive it with thankfulness and gladness. Help me to strengthen my commitment to you. Amen.

The Face of Christ

YOU MIGHT HAVE COME to the seashore hoping for a little God-and-me time, solitude to let you hear his voice in the gentle whisper of the sand and the rhythmic wash of the waves. If your vacation offers you time by yourself to contemplate his presence in his creation, by all means take it. But count it as a small part of your communion with your Lord, because communion with him unfolds and expands in your life with and among his people.

Mother Teresa once remarked that she saw Christ in the face of the poorest of the poor. In serving the poor, Mother Teresa communed with God every day, even though she lived and worked in the noisy and crowded slums of one of the most densely populated cities in the world. She saw God in others and served them, because through them she communed with Christ.

Through your relationships with others and your work among them, you commune with God. Maybe you don't see the poorest of the poor every day, but you do see your family, your friends, your coworkers, your boss, the person in front of you at the grocery checkout. Right now you see your traveling companions and fellow beachgoers. This evening's clambake brings even more faces bearing the face of Christ. Every person bears the image of their Creator, and when you're among people, you see the face of Christ.

You bear the face of Christ too. You have communion with God just by being you! And the wonderful thing about the communion you have with him is that you don't have to flee to a beach

hideaway, climb a remote mountain, or retreat to a barren wilderness to enjoy it. He is wherever you are.

Some God-and-me time lifts and refreshes the weary soul, but for a go-anywhere communion with God, open your eyes to the face of Christ in everyone you see.

> *No one has ever seen God; but if we love one another,*
> *God lives in us and his love is made complete in us.*
> 1 John 4:12

> *Where two or three come together in my name, there am I with them.*
> Matthew 18:20

THE ONLY BASIS FOR REAL FELLOWSHIP
WITH GOD *and* MAN IS TO LIVE
OUT IN THE OPEN WITH BOTH.

Roy Hession

Heavenly Father: I know it's true—sometimes I bundle myself up in you, but it's just an excuse for not dealing with others. Remind me that you love my brothers and sisters in the faith as much as you love me. Help me to always be open with them, cherishing the benefits each of them bring to my life. As I grow closer to them, I know I'll be growing closer to you. Thank you, Lord, for showing me the way. Amen.

Swimming Lessons

THEIR FIRST TIME AT THE BEACH, most little kids retreat in fear
when the foamy lip of a wave rolls in and laps at their toes. But
along comes Dad to lift his daughter high on his shoulders as he
wades out into the water. Daughter no longer panics but watches in
fascination as Dad maneuvers through the fearsome force beneath
her. Then her big brother announces that he knows how to swim.
In the surf he sprints, loudly showing off to his sister until the
next wave knocks him down. He emerges from the water dazed and
with a mouthful of saltwater. Mom soothes his shaken ego and
proceeds to teach her son how to navigate through the surf.

Perhaps you can relate to the kids. You know what it's like
to fear the sea, to avoid something God has put on your heart to
do. You lack confidence in your ability to handle the task, and
you'd just as soon let someone else jump in. Then God picks you
up and carries you into deep water. Your heavenly Father would no
more push you into a task you couldn't handle than would a loving parent toss a small child into the ocean. He leads you into the
task. He lets you watch others who have more experience. Perhaps
he sends someone to mentor you until you're confident enough
and strong enough to swim on your own.

Likewise, he's there for you when too much confidence lands
you flat on your backside and tasting salt. Jesus' disciple Peter suffered the indignity of overconfidence when a wave of doubt
overcame his ability to walk on water and he fell in. There's no
record of Jesus laughing (though he might have); it is recorded,

however, that Jesus rescued Peter. So get up, spit out the saltwater, and let Jesus show you how to swim!

Big ocean? Tall waves? No problem when you put your confidence in God.

Such confidence as this is ours through Christ before God. Not that we are competent in ourselves to claim anything for ourselves, but our competence comes from God.
2 Corinthians 3:4-5

I PLACE NO HOPE IN MY STRENGTH,
NOR IN MY WORKS:
but ALL MY CONFIDENCE IS IN GOD.
François Rabelais

Heavenly Father: You've given me a big job to do. I'm lying here on this sandy beach supposedly resting. But instead I'm worrying. How will I ever pull it off—do what you've called me to do. I feel so overwhelmed by the sheer greatness of it all. Help me, Lord, to place my trust in you and draw my confidence from your strength and capability. Amen.

Here's Looking at You

A SUNNY DAY AT THE BEACH is a people-watcher's paradise. Kids building a sand castle complete with a moat that fills as the tide rolls in, high schoolers caught up in a lively game of sand volleyball, young couples strolling hand in hand, moms and dads juggling five hot dogs and as many sodas across the hot sand to their beach-blanket spot. Just by watching, you can tell a great deal about the people. You see them being kind, gentle, playful, romantic, and caring. You can't see, however, whether they are Christians.

On the outside a Christian's life resembles the life of any person of goodwill. Obey the law. Respect others. Behave appropriately. Keep a positive attitude. You sunbathe, swim, picnic, toss a ball, and build sand castles, just like a lot of other people on vacation at the beach. Your motivation, however, differentiates you—a Christian—from others enjoying the same activities you are. God's Spirit leads you, as a Christian, to respond joyfully to the fantastic day the Lord has made. You receive the day as a blessing and a gift and use it well. And at the close of the day, you say a hearty "Thank you!" not to good luck or happy chance but to God.

In addition, you do thoughtful things for other people. You're caring and kind, just like any other good-hearted person. Motivated by God's Spirit, however, you do these things not to earn points but because you know how much God has already done for you. You acknowledge that he has given you your life and all the blessings you enjoy each day. You rely on him for help in challenging times and for comfort in troubling times. Because you do, you're motivated to extend his love to others. And that, in a seashell, is what the Christian life is all about.

> Set an example for the believers in speech,
> in life, in love, in faith and in purity.
> 1 Timothy 4:12

> This is how we know what love is: Jesus Christ laid down his life
> for us. And we ought to lay down our lives for our brothers.
> 1 John 3:16

BE SUCH A MAN, AND LIVE SUCH A LIFE,
THAT IF EVERY MAN *were* SUCH AS YOU,
AND EVERY LIFE A LIFE LIKE YOURS,
THIS EARTH WOULD BE GOD'S PARADISE.
Phillips Brooks

Dear Father: Most of all, I want my life to be pleasing to you. Then may it be an example to others of your goodness, since it's your name I carry. I want so much to be like you. Become great in me that I might live more fully for you. Amen.

A Grain of Sand

ENGLISH POET WILLIAM BLAKE opened "Auguries of Innocence" with the widely quoted lines, "To see a world in a grain of sand, and a heaven in a wild flower." Something as gigantic as a whole world contained in something as small as a grain of sand? The majesty of heaven in a single flower? Blake's paradoxical images point to the sacred wonder of all things created and the profound interconnectedness of all creation.

To illustrate his point, scoop up some sand. How you treat the grains of sand you hold in your hand reflects your attitude toward the whole of creation. For example, when you see litter on the beach, you pick it up and throw it away. Why? So shore birds won't swallow and choke on plastic soda-holder rings. So aluminum flip tops won't get caught on seagulls' beaks. So indigestible sandwich wrappers won't sicken fish. So you and anyone coming after you can enjoy a tranquil and pristine scene today. A small thing, picking up a piece of debris on a small patch of sand, but it says everything about your love for the whole earth.

Upon creating the world and everything in it, God pronounced it "good." He made the earth for people to live on, cultivate, explore, and enjoy. He also commanded people to take care of what he had made, to be good stewards of all he had created. Good and godly stewardship compels God's people to get involved in environmental issues, to teach and practice responsible use of the resources of earth, sea, and sky. Your stewardship of creation means that you take your caretaker role seriously. It means that you see the interconnectedness of all creation, starting with a grain of sand.

Look up into the heavens. Who created all the stars? He brings them out one after another, calling each by its name. And he counts them to see that none are lost or have strayed away.... Have you never heard or understood? Don't you know that the Lord is the everlasting God, the Creator of all the earth? He never grows faint or weary. No one can measure the depths of his understanding.
Isaiah 40:26, 28 NLT

THE MORE WE LEARN ABOUT THE WONDERS
OF OUR UNIVERSE, *the* MORE CLEARLY
WE ARE GOING TO PERCEIVE THE HAND OF GOD.
Frank Borman

Dear Father: I stand in awe of your creation. All around me I see your glory and majesty. Show me, Lord, how I can best show respect for you by honoring the work of your hands. Thank you for placing me in such a beautiful world—a world you created from nothing and sustain with your Word. Amen.

Good Picks

Discernment may sound like some sort of mystical skill, but it isn't. You used discernment when you planned your vacation. You thought about different places you could go and other beaches you could visit. You planned how long you would be gone from home and decided how much you could spend for a hotel room. You figured out how you would travel to the beach and how you would return home. You consulted with others to get their opinions and insight. You listened to a friend who had been to this beach before. You explored the Web sites of several resorts and checked out their vacation packages. In planning your vacation, you discerned the best options among the choices available to you.

To a point, discernment in spiritual matters works the same way. You want to grow in closeness to God and mature in your relationship with him. To do so, you must discern among the various spirits out there. The spirit of the age that urges you to do whatever feels right to you. The spirit of humanism that suggests you accept as true only what you can humanly understand. The Spirit of God—yes, this is it!—but which God? Now comes the point where unaided discernment fails. To help you discern the true God, the Holy Spirit enters your heart and plants faith.

As your faith grows, you begin to discern more and more about God, his will, and his work in you. You choose his Word from among all others held out to you, and you pick out his promises from among those the world dangles in front of you. You seek

advice from other Christians and learn from those who have traveled before you. And here you are, on the journey of a lifetime and for a lifetime as a wise and discerning disciple of Christ!

> *Preserve sound judgment and discernment,*
> *do not let them out of your sight;*
> *they will be life for you,*
> *an ornament to grace your neck.*
> Proverbs 3:21–22

> *I am your servant; give me discernment*
> *that I may understand your statutes.*
> Psalm 119:125

WISDOM COMES PRIVATELY FROM GOD
AS A BY-PRODUCT OF RIGHT DECISIONS,
GODLY REACTIONS, *and* THE APPLICATION
OF SPIRITUAL PRINCIPLES TO DAILY CIRCUMSTANCES.
Charles R. Swindoll

Heavenly Father: Thank you for giving me your Holy Spirit. Because he's with me, I'm able to effectively discern your will and your purpose for me. I can tell when it's your voice speaking to my heart. I can know what's true and what isn't. Teach me to listen carefully to your voice and choose wisely. Amen.

Guiding Star

THOUSANDS OF YEARS AGO, coastal people in various parts of the world ventured out into the seas. They fashioned vessels from hollowed-out logs, tied or woven reeds, or inflated animal hides. The first sailors navigated through the uncharted waters by using the sun and stars for direction. If the ancient sailors foolishly embarked on their journey without keeping their eyes on the skies for direction, they soon found themselves lost in the open seas with no idea where they were or where they were headed.

Discipleship means that you set out into life's uncharted waters the smart way—you keep your eyes on God for direction and follow where he leads. Your guiding star, Jesus Christ, keeps you on course. He presented the face of God to you by showing you his kindness, compassion, and mercy through his words and actions during the course of his ministry on earth. He proved the love of God for you by taking on himself the penalty for your sins through his suffering and death on the cross. He won a relationship with God for you through his resurrection from the grave. He lives now for you to help, guide, and support you in your journey through life.

Because of your discipleship, you need never be at a loss to know where you are or where you're headed. Though clouds may temporarily hide your guiding star from you, or storms may come between you and his light, you have his Word for direction. In times of darkness, let Jesus orient you toward him—read his promises of comfort and care. Point your life toward them and travel on in confidence.

Today, satellites rely on an onboard star tracker for positioning. Since you're away from city lights, perhaps you can spot one passing over the ocean tonight. As you gaze into the heavens, let the skies remind you that Christ is your center, your sun, your guiding star.

[Jesus said,] "My sheep listen to my voice; I know them, and they follow me."
John 10:27

Jesus said, "Anyone who does not take his cross and follow me is not worthy of me. Whoever finds his life will lose it, and whoever loses his life for my sake will find it."
Matthew 10:38–39

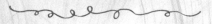

A DISCIPLE IS ONE WHO, REALIZING THE MEANING OF *the* ATONEMENT, DELIBERATELY GIVES HIMSELF UP TO JESUS CHRIST IN UNSPEAKABLE GRATITUDE.
Oswald Chambers

Heavenly Father: I want to be your disciple, following you wherever you lead, holding to your commandments, and listening for your voice. Receive my imperfect gift, my flawed effort, my tattered heart. As I follow you, purify, perfect, and heal me that I might be a worthy, obedient servant in your kingdom. Amen.

Fear Not

Watch kids coming to the beach. Some of them throw their beach towels on the sand and hit the water at a gallop. Others carefully arrange their towels, watch the waves a while, then timidly touch their toes to the surf. After all, the water's deep and the waves are tall. And there may be sharks! The more cautious kids scan the surface for circling fins, but when they see their friends bobbing in and out of the surf waving, hollering, and having fun, their fear fades away. They're encouraged to get in the water too.

Many times during his ministry on earth, Jesus greeted his disciples with the words "Fear not." With the same words he greets you. When you fear in front of his holiness out of shame or guilt, Jesus says, "Fear not my presence, because I've come to forgive, bless, comfort, and restore you." When you fear in the face of life's changes and uncertainties, Jesus says, "Fear not the world, because I've come to guide you through it." When you fear the difficulty of challenges ahead of you, Jesus says, "Fear not. Put your confidence in me. I encourage you to go ahead. Jump in. I'm here, right with you."

God encourages you to explore, discover, and persevere. He encourages you to confront challenges and take on opportunities. While he never advocates foolish risk, he helps you overcome fear that causes you to shy away from receiving all the blessings he has in store for you. He gives you the courage it takes to exercise your talents and skills, to come through your difficulties, and to take advantage of the opportunities open to you.

When you see other Christians making great strides in spiritual maturity and wisdom and enjoying life to the fullest, why let them have all the fun? Don't hesitate. Go ahead and jump right in!

Do not be fainthearted or afraid; do not be terrified....
For the LORD your God is the one who goes with you to fight
for you against your enemies to give you victory.
Deuteronomy 20:3-4

The LORD is my light and my salvation—whom shall I fear? The
LORD is the stronghold of my life—of whom shall I be afraid?
Psalm 27:1

MANY OF OUR FEARS ARE TISSUE-PAPER THIN,
and A SINGLE COURAGEOUS STEP WOULD
CARRY US CLEAR THROUGH THEM.
Brendan Francis

Dear Lord: I don't want to hold back—I want to dash forward, eager to experience everything you have in store for me. Strengthen, encourage, and fill me with courage as I take that first big step toward overcoming my fears and living life to the fullest. Thank you for being my Strong Tower in the midst of fearful surroundings. Amen.

A Sure Destination

WHEN SEAFARERS BEGAN TO EXPLORE the oceans of the world, they didn't know exactly what they would find at the end of their journey. New lands, a back door to their own country, an endless expanse of water, or a cliff off the edge of the world? It was far safer to sit on the shore and imagine what might lie just beyond the horizon than to launch out into the vast unknown. Only brave souls took on the seas.

Life's journey, however, offers no one the choice of lingering on the wharf. Everyone launches into life's hours and days, years and decades without knowing what lies ahead. And after this life? For some, "life after" stretches somewhere beyond the blurry horizon. They imagine pearly gates and streets of gold, another garden of Eden, a sheer drop into nothingness. Like the ancient seafarers, they travel with no certainty. But that's not what God intended.

If you have placed your faith in God and his Son, Jesus Christ, you not only have God's protection and guidance in this life's journey, but you know exactly where you're headed. The destination holds neither uncertainty nor fear for you. You're not going to fantasyland or fading into the sky. You're not destined to disappear into nothingness. As God's child, you're going to live with him and all the saints. You know for sure because he says so in his Word. At the end of your journey here, you'll live in a place of gladness and joy—a place Jesus called his Father's house. And you'll live in his Father's house forever. It's a promise.

God has done what you can never do: chart the course of your life with all its storms and smooth seas, islands and ports of call. Trust the Map Maker to see you safely to your destination— eternal life in heaven with him.

Surely goodness and love will follow me all the days of my life,
and I will dwell in the house of the LORD forever.
Psalm 23:6

[Jesus said,] "I tell you the truth, whoever hears my word and believes
him who sent me has eternal life and will not be condemned;
he has crossed over from death to life."
John 5:24

THE LIFE OF FAITH DOES NOT EARN ETERNAL LIFE;
IT IS ETERNAL LIFE. *And* CHRIST IS ITS VEHICLE.
William Temple

Dear Lord: What a gift! Eternal life. I can only imagine how it will be. But
I already know all I need to know. I know that I'll be where you are—in
your presence for eternity. Thank you, Lord, for your love. Your kindness
follows me every day of my life—and from here, the life to come. Amen.

Sand Castles

ALONG THE SHORE YOU COME ACROSS an elaborate sand castle. You admire the work of a master builder who has packed the sand with just the right amount of water and skillfully sculpted towers, turrets, rooms, and courtyards. Shells, pebbles, and pieces of driftwood adorn the royal domicile. You pass by the same place later, however, and you notice that the castle's gone. The tide has come in and with a few swooshes washed away the whole estate. Though cleverly, painstakingly, and beautifully built, the castle in the sand lacked permanence.

Jesus expects his people to build things that will last—things of permanence. During his ministry on earth, he frequently pointed out the importance of trust in God over reliance on self, of a humble prayer over grand oratory, of a teachable heart over a name in the world. Today, when you put God's commandments into practice in your life, you're building something permanent. His Word will never wash away, no matter how strong the tides against it. When you believe in Jesus Christ as your Lord and Savior, you're building something permanent. Your faith will never fail you, no matter how harsh the storms of life. And when you share the good news of God's love in Jesus Christ with someone, you're building something permanent—eternal, in fact—for the person in whom your words and example set the foundation for God-given faith.

Is it okay to build a sand castle? Of course. It's just that you know sand castles won't last—no matter how necessary you think

they are or how pleasing or decorative you find them—and you put eternal things first. When you do, everything else you need and want for this life falls into place. And the tides? You have nothing to fear. Your foundation rests secure in the everlasting Word of God.

[Jesus said,] "Everyone who hears these words of mine and puts them into practice is like a wise man who built his house on the rock. The rain came down, the streams rose, and the winds blew and beat against that house; yet it did not fall, because it had its foundation on the rock. But everyone who hears these words of mine and does not put them into practice is like a foolish man who built his house on sand. The rain came down, the streams rose, and the winds blew and beat against that house, and it fell with a great crash."
Matthew 7:24–27

LEARN TO HOLD LOOSELY ALL THAT IS NOT ETERNAL.
Agnes Maud Royden

Heavenly Father: I've worked so hard to build my life here on earth—the best education, the best job, the best house, the best car, the best investments, the best retirement plan. And yet in my heart of hearts I know that all those things will sooner or later wash away. They have no permanence. As I turn my heart toward eternal things, I pray that you would illuminate my mind. Help me to see the temporary and distinguish it from the lasting so that I might live my life here for you as well as prepare for my eternal life. Amen.

Under Construction

WALK ALONG THE MARINA and you might see someone repairing a boat or even building one. You watch a while, then continue on your stroll. But imagine walking along a desert road and seeing a man building a boat. Noticing that the man doesn't have a four-wheel drive vehicle equipped with a hitch to haul the boat to water, you wonder what in the world he had in mind when he started building.

Noah's neighbors had plenty to wonder about as they watched the old man build a barge on dry land. No doubt tongues wagged and heads shook in disbelief. Yet Noah continued with his peculiar project simply because God had told him to build an ark. Noah put his faith in God and ignored the opinions of wise guys. When the floods came, the fruit of Noah's faith—the ark—saved him and his family from destruction.

Your God-given faith in Jesus Christ puts you in Noah's position—in the desert building an ark. In the arid land of this world, you drink from the living waters of God's Word. As a result, you live by his moral and ethical standards. Sometimes you feel the sting of ridicule for not bowing to the latest "scientific" findings or for questioning the decency of certain TV shows and movies. Or maybe God has laid on your heart a task others find impossible or laughable. But you persevere in it. You continue building. Then when the floods come—the trials, the troubles, the traumas of life—your faith holds you up. Your faith sees you through.

Right now, you're on vacation, and you probably have no intention of building a boat. But rest assured, the Holy Spirit has

every intention of building firm, seaworthy, and storm-proof faith
in you!

> *Be on your guard; stand firm in the faith;*
> *be men of courage; be strong.*
> 1 Corinthians 16:13

> *Faith is being sure of what we hope for*
> *and certain of what we do not see.*
> Hebrews 11:1

THE GREATEST FAITH OF ALL, AND THE MOST
EFFECTIVE, IS TO LIVE DAY BY DAY TRUSTING [GOD].
IT IS TRUSTING HIM SO MUCH *that* WE LOOK
AT EVERY PROBLEM AS AN OPPORTUNITY
TO SEE HIS WORK IN OUR LIFE.
Rick Joyner

Lord God: I want the kind of faith that can endure any storm, but I know
that comes only as I follow you and grow in your ways. Take the faith I
have—my willingness to act on what you speak to me—and make it
strong and seaworthy. I trust you as I have never trusted anyone else.
Help me trust you more. Amen.

Of Huge Importance

OCCASIONALLY YOU READ ABOUT THE PLIGHT of a beached whale. Stranded in shallow water, the whale can become dehydrated and die, or the high tide can suffocate the mammal by blocking its blowhole. Many theories have attempted to explain this beaching phenomenon. Experts think it could be the result of pollution, natural changes in the earth's magnetic pull, or trauma caused by high-intensity ship sonar. What is undisputed, however, is this: A whale stranded for too long out of its element—water—dies.

Likewise, faith taken out of its element—association with other Christians—runs a high risk of dying as well. That's why the Bible talks so much about spending time in fellowship with other believers. Fellowship isn't just about coffee and doughnuts in the church hall; it's about receiving God's blessings and growing in faith. It's about being encouraged that others are experiencing—and overcoming—the same challenges you're facing. It's about having a human shoulder to cry on, someone you can lean on and pray with, someone to help you keep things in perspective. A beached faith misses out on these things. A beached faith risks suffocation.

Staying in fellowship also gives you the opportunity to encourage and sustain others, to allow your faith to inspire hope and endurance in your fellow believers during their moments of weakness and need.

In community with other Christians, you exercise the particular gifts God has given you, unique gifts that no one else has or uses in quite the same way. But unused gifts are like a job left undone, a task left incomplete, a "good morning" left unsaid. You can only be God's hands, feet, and heart to his people if you spend time with them. For the life and health of your faith, stay in your element. Remain in fellowship with the saints of God.

Let the word of Christ dwell in you richly as you teach and admonish one another with all wisdom, and as you sing psalms, hymns and spiritual songs with gratitude in your hearts to God.
Colossians 3:16

BE UNITED WITH OTHER CHRISTIANS.
A WALL WITH LOOSE BRICKS *is* NOT GOOD.
THE BRICKS MUST BE CEMENTED TOGETHER.
Corrie ten Boom

Heavenly Father: I wish I could say that I always enjoy being with other believers, but I don't. Sometimes it takes every bit of my patience. Then there are times when I feel out of sorts, unworthy, unlikable, so I stay away. I see now that I've been missing the bigger picture. We're a family, and families aren't perfect. Open my heart to receive as I am received, to love as I am loved, and to trust you through it all. Amen.

True Friend

Perhaps from where you're sitting, you can see a bridge or a causeway over the water. That bridge connects two points of land separated by a body of water. Human beings and God Almighty are like two points of land separated by a body of water—the treacherous, shark-infested water of sin. On God's side, holiness reigns. On this side, brokenness rules.

Jesus, God's Son, has closed the gap between God's holiness and your brokenness. He willingly "came over" to your side in the form of a man with flesh and bones, born of a woman in a certain place and at a particular time in history. In his ministry, he healed people and reached out to them in compassion and mercy. In his death, he took on himself the brokenness of the world and made holiness possible for all who believe in him. As your bridge between two worlds, Jesus made it possible for you to walk over to God. He made it possible for you to call God your friend.

Because of and through Jesus, you can approach God in prayer at any time. As your friend, Jesus invites you to tell him about anything that's on your heart. In fact, he urges you to do so, just as your best friend might say, "Really, I want you to tell me what's bothering you." As your friend, Jesus comforts and consoles you when you're down and stands with you when you need his support and encouragement, just as your best friend might tell you,

"I'm here for you"—and mean it. As your friend, Jesus tells you when you're wrong and gives you honest answers to your questions. Would you want your best friend to do anything else? You can find his guidance and his answers to your questions in his holy Word.

As your eternal friend, Jesus remains faithful to you not just for a lifetime but forever.

> *A man of many companions may come to ruin,*
> *but there is a friend who sticks closer than a brother.*
> Proverbs 18:24

> *[Jesus said,] "I no longer call you servants, because a servant does not*
> *know his master's business. Instead, I have called you friends, for*
> *everything that I learned from my Father I have made known to you."*
> John 15:15

THE DEAREST FRIEND ON EARTH *is* A MERE
SHADOW COMPARED WITH JESUS CHRIST.
Oswald Chambers

Dear Lord: What a wonderful privilege to be called your friend. I can barely take it in. And yet it's true; your Word says so. I want to reveal everything to you—my thoughts, feelings, dreams, hurts—just as I would to my dearest friend. Open my heart, cleanse and purify it, and receive me into your presence. Thank you for being the best friend I've ever had. Amen.

Treasures from the Sea

THE SEA IS GENEROUS. The rich array of shells adorning the shore offers you treasures to pick up and hold and carry in your pocket as mementos of a leisurely morning stroll. The joyous play of sunlight and moonlight across the water fills you with wonder and delight. Perhaps you've ridden in a glass-bottom boat or been scuba diving and discovered breathtaking coral reefs just below the water's surface. If so, you've had an experience you'll remember forever. While listening to the rhythmic ebb and flow of the tides, you've found comfort and rest. Yes, the seas are giving waters.

Like the ocean, the Christian life is a giving life. Jesus Christ set the example in his life, death, and resurrection. He gave himself completely for the sake of the world and the salvation of all who believe in him. It's no surprise, then, that those who follow him give, and give generously. They overflow with words and actions that shower others with kindness, respect, and compassion. They never hesitate to provide practical assistance wherever it's needed, and they work diligently to give everyone an opportunity to share the good things life has to offer. They're the ones who give not out of any thought of personal gain or recognition but merely because they saw Jesus Christ, their Savior, do it first.

Through these giving believers, God spreads his message of hope in Jesus Christ to a world in need of salvation, his comfort to a world in need of peace. Believers give others the good news of God's love by sharing his Word and his promises. The Christian life—your

life—is a giving life. Right before your eyes, the sea is giving you all the beauty and majesty it has to offer. Within you, Jesus is giving you himself so that you can give of yourself to others.

> *A generous man will prosper;*
> *he who refreshes others will himself be refreshed.*
> Proverbs 11:25

> *[Jesus said,] "Give, and it will be given to you. A good measure,*
> *pressed down, shaken together and running over, will be poured into*
> *your lap. For with the measure you use, it will be measured to you."*
> Luke 6:38

> GIVING IS THE SECRET OF A HEALTHY LIFE.
> NOT NECESSARILY MONEY, *but* WHATEVER
> A MAN HAS OF ENCOURAGEMENT AND
> SYMPATHY AND UNDERSTANDING.
> *John D. Rockefeller Jr.*

Dear Father: I think of myself as a generous person, but I know I could give much more—more smiles, more encouragement, more pats on the shoulder, more love. Help me each day to be a fitting example of your generous nature, giving to others from a heart of gratitude because you have given so much to me. Amen.

Master of All

MASSIVE WAVES CRASHING ONTO SHORE have a way of asserting the authority of the sea. If you're unconvinced, just wade into the surf and wait for the next big wave. If it doesn't knock you flat on your backside, the next one surely will. Sorry, but when you're in the sea's domain, the sea is stronger and it has the authority.

Guess who has authority over the entire world? That's right—God! But a lot of people just don't want to believe that authority rests anywhere except with themselves. They grab control of their lives, health, money, careers, and possessions. They get knocked down again and again. Plans go wrong. Health falters. Investments plummet in value. Possessions fail to satisfy.

God asserts his authority over you because he loves you. His commandments curb the destructive desires of your human mind and flesh. By obeying him and putting yourself under the authority of his Word, you avoid getting knocked down by the negative consequences of poor choices and dead-end decisions. The authority of his gospel— Jesus' message of redemption and grace—keeps you afloat when trials and troubles would otherwise knock you flat. Because you believe in the authority of his promises and his power to follow through on them, you find comfort, contentment, and peace in situations where others find only the swirl of confusion and chaos.

Been knocked down a few times? That's okay. God knows—he really does!—that his children get themselves into deep water sometimes. Just remember who has the authority, the will, and the power to pull you to shore.

Praise be to the name of God for ever and ever; wisdom and power are his. He changes times and seasons; he sets up kings and deposes them. He gives wisdom to the wise and knowledge to the discerning. He reveals deep and hidden things; he knows what lies in darkness, and light dwells with him.

Daniel 2:20–22

Wealth and honor come from you; you are the ruler of all things. In your hands are strength and power to exalt and give strength to all. Now, our God, we give you thanks, and praise your glorious name.

1 Chronicles 29:12–13

THOSE WHO WALK IN GOD'S SHADOW
ARE NOT THREATENED *by* THE STORM.
Andrea Garney

Dear Lord: I've learned the hard way that my decisions are flawed when I leave you out of them. They are often shortsighted because they haven't been guided by you—the one who sees and knows all. Forgive me for choosing my own limited understanding rather than your ageless wisdom. Help me remember to call on you in every decision I make. Amen.

Carefree

IN ANSWER TO A SCHOLAR'S QUESTION, Jesus told the parable of the good Samaritan. The Samaritan, unlike other passersby, had compassion on a man who lay on the roadway robbed, beaten, and bleeding. The Samaritan's compassion led to him to offer practical help. He bandaged the man's wounds, placed the man on his donkey, and took him to an inn. Since the man couldn't pay, the Samaritan paid the bill and gave the innkeeper his promise to take care of any additional expenses on his return trip.

Sin beats and wounds every human being, yet most people walk by quickly and look the other way when they see someone bruised and bleeding as a consequence of sin. God doesn't. Like the Samaritan in Jesus' parable, Jesus has compassion on you, and his compassion results in practical help. He pours the ointment of forgiveness on your wounded heart to bring about healing and restore you to wholeness. Though others have abandoned you, he picks you up in his arms and takes you to the refuge of his Word and the shelter of his promises. His Word encourages you to rely on him, trust in him, and grow in him as you prepare to get up and walk again. His promises assure you of his good plans for you and of his abiding presence in your life.

And the bill? God knows you can't pay—no one can—so he paid it for you. Jesus, by his death on the cross, paid the price for all sin and every wound that sin ever has and ever will inflict. You have nothing to worry about when it comes to paying. He promised to take care of the bill—and he has.

Perhaps right now you're stretched out on the beach without a care in the world, and loving every minute of it. That's great! And you can love every minute of your life because God cares for you.

[Jesus said,] "What's the price of a pet canary? Some loose change, right? And God cares what happens to it even more than you do. He pays even greater attention to you, down to the last detail—even numbering the hairs on your head! So don't be intimidated by all this bully talk. You're worth more than a million canaries."
Matthew 10:29–31 MSG

The LORD is good to those whose hope is in him, to the one who seeks him; it is good to wait quietly for the salvation of the Lord.
Lamentations 3:25–26

THE LORD MY PASTURE SHALL PREPARE, AND FEED ME WITH A SHEPHERD'S CARE; HIS PRESENCE SHALL MY WANTS SUPPLY, *and* GUARD ME WITH A WATCHFUL EYE.
Joseph Addison

Precious heavenly Father: When I consider how you care for me, hearing every prayer, often answering—as your Word says—even before I ask, protecting me from harm and providing for my needs, my heart is filled with love for you. Thank you for your loving care. You're an awesome God! Amen.

Good Sense

To get an idea of the ocean's character, you use your senses. You see its size—gigantic. You hear the peaceful rhythm of gentle surf and the restless roar of choppy waves, and you appreciate the ocean's complexity. You dip your hand in and determine whether the water is warm or cold. You lick your finger and taste its saltiness. You breathe in the sea air.

In the same way, to get an idea of God's character, he invites you to use your senses. You see the majesty of earth, sky, and seas and conclude that the Creator must be powerful and possess a sense of order and beauty. You hear his Word, in which you learn about his work in the lives of his people and all he has done on their behalf throughout history. You listen as God tells you he loves you and has sent his Son, Jesus, to make a relationship with him possible. From all this, you realize that God has shown he's merciful, loving, and self-sacrificing. In the kindly touch of another person, the warm embrace of a loved one, and the secure grasp of another's hand in yours, you experience God's care for you and about you in everyday life. At the communion table, in fellowship with other believers, you taste his promises as he forgives sins and strengthens faith.

Now you may be wondering how smell fits in, but that's easy. The Bible compares the heartfelt prayers of God's people to the sweet aroma of incense. So go ahead—

pray, breathe deeply, and take pleasure in the fragrance, because God delights in hearing from you. And if you find that any of your spiritual senses need sharpening, ask another believer to tell you more about God's amazing character. God, beyond understanding, wants to make himself known to you and invites you to know him.

> *O taste and see that the LORD is good:*
> *blessed is the man that trusteth in him.*
> Psalm 34:8 KJV

> *The LORD is good,*
> *a refuge in times of trouble.*
> *He cares for those who trust in him.*
> Nahum 1:7

MAN IS A SPIRITUAL BEING, *and* THE PROPER
WORK OF HIS MIND IS TO INTERPRET THE WORLD
ACCORDING TO HIS HIGHER NATURE.
Robert Bridges

Oh, Father: Open my heart to know you—to see, hear, and feel you. Teach me to see you working all around me, to hear your voice speaking to me through your Word and whispering insights to my heart, to feel your presence within me, closer than my breath. Thank you for the privilege of experiencing your greatness in my life. Amen.

Grace-full Living

"IF ONE LIVES A LONG TIME immersed in God's grace," someone has observed, "there stretches across one's soul a calm which nothing can destroy."

After many days at the beach, you're immersed in its rhythm, its ebb and flow, its shadows and tides. You've long forgotten what's going on back home, and you've pushed far back in your mind the tensions that test your patience at work. Maybe you find great peace in walking by yourself along the shore in the cool, crisp air of morning. Perhaps you venture out beyond the breaking waves, lie on a raft, and blissfully let the gently rocking, sun-dappled water cradle you. The lines disappear from between your brows. Your mouth relaxes to a gentle smile. Your neck and shoulders lose the knots you've tried in vain to get rid of with exercise and massages. If your friends could see you now, they'd exclaim, "You look so relaxed! How did you do it?"

You'd respond, "The ocean did it. Just being in its presence gives me peace."

When you immerse yourself in God's grace, expect to see—and others to see—changes in the way you look and the way you act. How do you find God's grace? It comes only by faith in him. When you read, study, and meditate on his Word, you soak up his grace. When, in life's trials and challenges, you rest on his promise to hold you up under all circumstances, you're immersed in his grace. It won't be long before tension disappears, stress evaporates, and your body relaxes in the deep pool of your spiritual tranquillity. You'll notice. Your family, friends, and coworkers will notice. They may want to know what book you're reading or what exercises you're doing. What a perfect time to lead them to the shore of God's free and abundant grace!

To each one of us grace has been given as Christ apportioned it.
Ephesians 4:7

God is able to make all grace abound to you, so that in all things at all times, having all that you need, you will abound in every good work.
2 Corinthians 9:8

GRACE MEANS THE FREE, UNMERITED,
UNEXPECTED LOVE OF GOD, AND ALL THE BENEFITS,
DELIGHTS, *and* COMFORTS WHICH FLOW FROM IT.
IT MEANS THAT WHILE WE WERE SINNERS AND ENEMIES
WE HAVE BEEN TREATED AS SONS AND HEIRS.
R. P. C. Hanson

Heavenly Father: Thank you for your gift of grace poured out on me through the sacrifice your Son, Jesus, made on the cross. I don't deserve your love, kindness, forgiveness, and loving care—and yet it's mine. You give me everything I need. As I rest in that grace, help me surrender completely to you, releasing all my stress, unloading all my burdens into your open arms. Amen.

Lifeguard on Duty

SAD BUT TRUE: A panicked swimmer often fights a rescuer and can cause both to drown. Water-safety rules advise you to throw a flotation device to the person or, better yet, alert the lifeguard and phone for an emergency-rescue team.

Spiritual panic—fear of personal failure, distress over unfortunate choices of your own or a loved one, grief over illness and loss—can cause you to struggle against the one who comes to rescue you. After all, you're a mature adult, able to manage your own resources, circumstances, and emotions. You do most things successfully and well. People who know you and work with you say you're a strong swimmer. And strong swimmers don't drown, right? But statistics scream "Wrong!" Even strong swimmers can find themselves in distress and danger. Their muscles may give out against a strong current that pulls them out to sea. Stomach cramps can render them unable to stay afloat. Or they may unwittingly step into an underwater precipice and find themselves in water far deeper than they can manage. Another danger strong swimmers face is overconfidence. A strong, experienced swimmer may take risks, such as surfing on a stormy day or going in the water alone on an unguarded beach.

Do you ever find yourself struggling in some of the deep waters of life? If so, it simply means that you need some help staying afloat and getting back to shore. After you get back to shore, you might think about what happened so that you can avoid the same situation next time. But when you're in the midst of water that's way over your head, don't struggle against God. He has come to rescue you. Take the life preserver he offers you and rely on his power to help you. He's one lifeguard who's always on duty, and he has the strength to bring you safely to shore. Let him do that for you, okay?

[You] are being protected by the power of God through faith for a salvation ready to be revealed in the last time.
1 Peter 1:5 NRSV

Be strong in the LORD and in his mighty power.
Ephesians 6:10

GREAT IS THE LORD, HIS PRESENCE INFINITE, ...
HIS BRIGHTNESS INSUPPORTABLE, HIS MAJESTY
AWFUL, *his* DOMINION BOUNDLESS,
AND HIS SOVEREIGNTY INCONTESTABLE.
MATTHEW HENRY

Great heavenly Father: I praise you for your greatness. I surrender myself to your goodness, kindness, and righteousness. Take hold of me and pull me out of this watery circumstance; lift me up and put my feet back on dry land. Help me not to struggle against your discipline, against your wise dealing in my life. Without you, I would be lost. Amen.

Souvenirs

WALK INTO ONE OF THE SOUVENIR SHOPS lining the boardwalk, and you'll find an array of items you can take home. You might choose a scenic postcard and a shell magnet for the refrigerator door, or a piece of driftwood art for your desk. Or maybe a T-shirt with the resort's name emblazoned on the back. Though you can't take the ocean home with you, you can take home a few favorite souvenirs and many happy memories of your great vacation at the beach.

Some people collect favorite souvenirs and happy memories of great vacations with God. A childhood Bible reminds them of their innocent promise to love God forever. A program from a Christmas Eve church service evokes heartwarming memories of family times together. A unique cross pendant from a recent retreat prompts thoughts of the friends they made that week. You might have some of those things tucked away in a dresser drawer or a storage box at home. But if all you take back from an encounter with God are souvenirs and memories, you're missing the point.

Unlike the ocean, you can take God back home with you. No need to divide vacation time from home time, because God is present all the time. Of course, you're blessed if you can experience him more intensely or see him more clearly when you celebrate a religious milestone in your life, worship with others at a festive time of year, or go to a place where you can meditate on his Word without the distractions of everyday life. And it's always good to keep favorite souvenirs and happy memories to remind you of the special way he made himself known to you at a particular time in your life. But remember that God isn't like the immovable ocean. He's your ever-present God. So when you go home, be sure to take him with you.

> *[Jesus said,] "Be sure of this: I am with you always,*
> *even to the end of the age."*
> Matthew 28:20 NLT

> *No one shall be able to stand against you all the days of your life.*
> *As I was with Moses, so I will be with you;*
> *I will not fail you or forsake you.*
> Joshua 1:5 NRSV

> $\mathcal{G}$OD, WHO IS EVERYWHERE,
> NEVER LEAVES US. YET HE SEEMS
> SOMETIMES *to* BE PRESENT, SOMETIMES ABSENT.
> *Thomas Merton*

Dear Father: I know that you're always with me. Even when I don't feel you, you're there. Teach me, Lord, to have a greater awareness of your presence, to feel you, acknowledge you, and honor you continually. I'm so glad to have you with me, and I know that you will stay, now and forever. Amen.

Marked by His Promises

IN A COASTAL CITY a tourist approached a resident and said, "I'm lost. I'm staying with a friend who lives in an apartment on a street lined with palm trees. Can you tell me where it is?"

You guessed it: Palm trees lined every street and boulevard for several blocks around. The exotic appearance of the stately trees had made one street distinctive to the tourist. Among many such streets, however, rows of palm trees provided no distinguishing mark at all.

If you believe simply that there is a God, you'll find yourself wandering around in a world of many beliefs in God. The natural world attests to the existence of a god. The human spirit yearns for the power of a god. Believing "there is a God" puts you in the presence of a god with no distinguishing marks. Should you need to ask for directions to this god, you'll hear a different answer from everyone you ask.

In contrast, the God of the Bible reveals himself to you so that you'll know exactly what sets him apart from every other god. He distinguishes himself by his promises, beginning with his promise to save a fallen world from the consequences of sin. He made good this promise in the person of Jesus Christ, who lived, died, and rose again to win your salvation. Before ascending into heaven, Jesus promised to send his disciples his Spirit. In fulfillment of Jesus' promise, the Holy Spirit came and empowered the disciples to teach and preach the gospel to all people.

God's promises still hold true for believers today. He promises to comfort you when you're in distress, to strengthen your faith when you're in doubt, and to give you peace in the midst of life's turbulence and troubles.

If you're lost, ask about the God of promises—the one with the will and the power to keep them.

God has made a great many promises. They are all "Yes" because of what Christ has done. So through Christ we say "Amen."
2 Corinthians 4:20 NIRV

You know with all your heart and soul that not one of all the good promises the LORD your God gave you has failed. Every promise has been fulfilled; not one has failed.
Joshua 23:14

THERE IS A LIVING GOD; HE HAS SPOKEN *in* THE BIBLE. HE MEANS WHAT HE SAYS AND WILL DO ALL HE HAS PROMISED.
Hudson Taylor

Dear Father: Thank you for your promises. Such a great and mighty God as you certainly doesn't owe me anything—especially not your promises. And yet you've given them—many of them—in the Bible, your Letter to me. Most of all, you've promised to forgive me, love me, and allow me to live in your presence for eternity. I owe you all my praise. Amen.

Signs in the Sand

ON MANY BEACHES YOU'LL SEE SIGNS posted in the sand. These signs signal warnings about hazardous tides and threatening weather conditions. If you fail to learn what the symbols mean, you risk putting yourself in a perilous situation. And you may well find yourself a victim, even though you've been warned of the hazard.

God also posts warning signs to protect you from potential dangers. He sets his signs right in front of you so you can't miss seeing them. But you need to read his signs and learn what they mean so you can benefit from the protection he offers you. Some of his signs come in the form of local and national laws. Through the laws of the land, God protects you from acts that could threaten your safety. But most of his signs are in the Bible. In his commandments God protects you from offenses and attitudes that endanger your relationship with him and with others.

Perhaps there's a sign or two you've chosen to ignore, a warning posted that you figured didn't apply to you. Sometimes it takes a perilous situation to demonstrate just how important God's signs are. But while rip currents, hurricanes, and killer waves aren't very forgiving, God is. When you turn to him in repentance, he welcomes you back with open arms. His Spirit renews his work in you and restores your relationship with him. You also gain an added respect for signs and their meaning. You've found out that his signs are meant not to put restrictions around your life but to point you to a joyful and fulfilling life under his strong, protective hand.

Now that you know about God's signs, help others read and understand them. And if you're unsure what the signs along the beach mean, ask someone who knows. The information could save your life.

The Lord is the one who keeps you safe. So let the Most High God be like a home to you. Then no harm will come to you. No terrible plague will come near your tent. The Lord will command his angels to take good care of you.
Psalm 91:9–11 NIRV

The Lord is faithful, and he will strengthen and protect you from the evil one.
2 Thessalonians 3:3

THIS IS A WISE, SANE CHRISTIAN FAITH: THAT A MAN COMMIT HIMSELF, HIS LIFE, AND HIS HOPES TO GOD; THAT GOD UNDERTAKES *the* SPECIAL PROTECTION OF THAT MAN; THAT THEREFORE THAT MAN OUGHT NOT TO BE AFRAID OF ANYTHING.
George MacDonald

Dear Father: There have been times when I've ignored your warnings. I was just too caught up in the excitement of the moment or my own vain desires to listen. I guess that means I'm human. But I do ask, Lord, that you would teach me to pray before I act, to listen before I rush ahead. Life is too dangerous to carelessly run out ahead of your loving hand of protection. Thank you for teaching me to be diligent in heeding your loving words of warning. Amen.

Fishy Gifts

EACH MORNING FISHING ENTHUSIASTS stake out a space at the end of the pier. With fishing poles propped against tackle boxes, some sit in folding chairs and gaze out over the water as they wait for the fish to bite. Others grip their poles and stare at the water below, impatient for the telltale tug of a hooked fish. Watching them, perhaps you're reminded of the saying, "Give a man a fish, and you've fed him for one day. Teach him to fish, and you've fed him for a lifetime."

Did you realize that God provides for you both ways? Sometimes he plops a fish in your lap. A real windfall, more than you ever dreamed of, comes out of nowhere. It's a basket of fish you know you haven't earned and suspect you don't deserve, but there it is. God has showered a blessing on you to use and enjoy today. So take it, thank him for it, and delight in it. He created the fish, and he can give it to whomever he pleases. And it pleased him to give the gift to you.

Most often, though, God provides for you by teaching you how to fish. He has given you particular abilities and talents (unearned and undeserved gifts in themselves!) and presents you with opportunities to use them for your benefit and the benefit of others. Through the use of these God-given gifts, you'll be fed for a lifetime. Your ability to study and acquire knowledge offers you a lifetime of discovery and accomplishment. The daily employment of your skills strengthens your family and builds the resources you need for a lifetime of stability and self-sufficiency.

When you see someone with a fishing pole baited and ready

to reel in the big one, think about the big ones God has given you. Think, too, about the big ones God has taught you how to catch. Thank and praise him mightily for both!

> *[God] has shown kindness by giving you rain from heaven*
> *and crops in their seasons; he provides you with plenty*
> *of food and fills your hearts with joy.*
> Acts 14:17

THERE IS NO NEED TOO GREAT FOR GOD.
HE HAS UNLIMITED RESOURCES *at* HIS DISPOSAL,
AND HE DELIGHTS IN MAKING THEM
AVAILABLE TO HIS CHILDREN.
Meriwether Williams

Good and gracious Father: Thank you for those times when you've just given me gifts. There are more than I can number, and you know I'm grateful for every one. I also want to thank you for the times when you've used my needs to teach me. You were always there ready to act, but you let me work and pray and use my gifts. I came away with a new level of confidence, enhanced faith, and a sense of accomplishment. You're so good to me, providing all I need and allowing me to grow in the process. Amen.

It's About Time

"Have a good time!" Perhaps you heard those words more than once as you prepared to leave on your vacation. You'd been anticipating your time off, and now that you're here, you expect to have a good time. "It's about time," you say to yourself as you stretch out in the sand. Yes, it's about time.

The rhythm of the waves on the shore stretches back to the beginning of time and will continue to the end of time. The tides of the ancient waters ebb and flow today and will do so until the Lord comes again in glory. Without a doubt, God created for the long haul. He created time and he has time. His timing rules the seas, the seasons—and you.

It's human nature to want things immediately, and in many instances God says, "Yes. Go ahead. You can have it right now." But the God who created time also says, "Wait. Wait until you can handle it. Wait until you reach the next stage of your life. Wait, I have something else for you. Wait on my timing. Wait on me."

Leave the attempts to jump back in time to writers of science fiction and directors of fantasy movies. Resist the impulse to rush ahead and get what you can right now. Instead, look out over the great waters of the sea. Hear the waves lap against the shore. No matter what happened or didn't happen in the past, yesterday is gone. No matter what will happen or won't happen in the future, tomorrow isn't here yet. God has given you today.

When you get back home and you feel the pressure to rush time, to hurry through time, to regret lost time, to long for better times, remember what you're seeing and hearing right now. Let the timeless peace of the ocean fill your soul. Breathe deeply of its ageless tranquillity. Trust God with your time and have a great time every day of your life.

I trust in you, O LORD; I say, "You are my God."
My times are in your hands.
Psalm 31:14–15

[God] has made everything beautiful in its time. He has also set eternity in the hearts of men; yet they cannot fathom what God has done from beginning to end.
Ecclesiastes 3:11

TRUST IN GOD AND YOU ARE NEVER to BE CONFOUNDED IN TIME OR ETERNITY.
Dwight L. Moody

Dear Lord: I know I'm impatient. I hate waiting, and I want everything to happen right away. I want what I want when I want it. But I know that tendency in me isn't part of my new sanctified nature. It causes me to make hasty and often improper choices. And that's not all. It indicates that I'm still struggling with pride and ego. Forgive me, Lord, and teach me to live in submission to your perfect timing. Amen.

Shallow Pools and Rough Waters

ALONG SOME COASTLINES you'll discover sheltered beaches. The shallow pool of gently rippling water epitomizes serenity. Marine researchers, however, have found that sheltered beaches harbor high levels of harmful bacteria because the waters aren't regularly replenished by the tides. The tranquillity of sheltered beaches comes with a price—contamination.

Some believers want to keep God's Word confined and protected like a sheltered beach. With worthy intentions, these believers guard God's holiness and the purity of his message by cutting it off from the skepticism, antagonism, and outright disbelief of the world. As with the waters of a sheltered beach, however, enclosure poses risks. Harmful microorganisms find a favorable breeding ground in pools shut off from the sea. When believers keep God's message to themselves, the sins of pride, self-importance, and exclusivity begin to breed. When believers restrict God's Word to an hour of Sunday worship and ten minutes of daily prayer, they never test his truths against the claims of the world. They don't know whether faith really works. Doubt in God's power and effectiveness in the real world grows.

God never intended his Word to become a sheltered beach where believers go to escape the world's complexity. While his Word offers you a respite from the world, it also provides you with strength and power to face the world. Life's storms and stresses give you opportunities to find out for yourself that God's Word is true and really works. As you face the tough questions, pointed challenges, and antagonism of the world toward God's Word and search its pages for answers, your faith is nourished and replenished.

With a word from his mouth, God created the sea. With his Word in your heart, you can handle calm or stormy seas.

All Scripture is God-breathed and is useful for teaching, rebuking, correcting and training in righteousness, so that the man of God may be thoroughly equipped for every good work.
2 Timothy 3:16–17

THE BIBLE DOES NOT THRILL, THE BIBLE
NOURISHES. GIVE TIME TO THE READING
of THE BIBLE, AND THE RECREATING EFFECT IS
AS REAL AS THAT OF FRESH AIR PHYSICALLY.
Oswald Chambers

Dear Father: Thank you for your Word, the Bible. As I read, open my heart to receive the truths I find there. May I not only find truth but live it, proving that your Word is every bit as perfect as you are. When I find passages I don't understand, I will come to you for wisdom, ask other believers for their insights, and open my mind to learn from you. Amen.

Gifts of Creation

MANY BEACHES OFFER BOAT EXCURSIONS into coastal waters. If you're lucky, during a trip you'll see a party of dolphins leaping, splashing, and playing. You might even spot a few whales surfacing for air. And you're sure to enjoy the sight of seagulls and grebes circling overhead and the dappled play of sunlight on the water around you. As you take in the wonder of nature, your appreciation for the marvels of creation moves you to offer a prayer of thanksgiving to the Creator of it all.

Time away from familiar surroundings heightens your appreciation for the world around you. Fresh to all your senses, this corner of creation amazes and excites you. But what if you took that appreciation back home and looked out your front window with the same eyes of amazement? What if you simply stood and watched a flock of feisty sparrows squabble at the feeder, or a bed of feathery clouds float across a patch of sky? What if you stooped to smell a summer rose, reached out to touch an autumn leaf, or stopped to mindfully breathe in the crisp, fresh air of approaching winter? What if you put your hand on new spring grass and felt the cool, moist leaves, or stuck your tongue out to catch a raindrop?

Right now, spectacular sights all around you compel you to fully appreciate God's amazing creation. But when you return home, you'll still be surrounded and blessed by his handiwork. Whether it's a sliver of sky between apartment buildings or a couple hundred acres of corn growing out back, geraniums in a

window box or a meadow of wildflowers, you'll be looking at a miracle and an astounding testament to life. You'll realize with a heart full of gratitude that creation everywhere is nothing less than a marvelous thing.

O give thanks to the LORD, call on his name, make known his deeds among the peoples. Sing to him, sing praises to him, tell of all his wonderful works.
1 Chronicles 16:8–9 NRSV

Praise the LORD! I will give thanks to the LORD with my whole heart, in the company of the upright, in the congregation. Great are the works of the LORD, studied by all who delight in them.
Psalm 111:1–2 NRSV

GRATITUDE TO GOD MAKES *even* A TEMPORAL BLESSING A TASTE OF HEAVEN.
William Romaine

Oh, Lord: My heart is overflowing with gratitude for all you've done— for the wonders of your creation and the marvelous nature of your grace. I thank you for your hand of mercy and your heart of unfailing love. I'm so grateful, Lord. Words aren't adequate to describe your goodness, but my soul will sing your praises forever. Amen.

It's Only Natural

IT'S A NATURAL TENDENCY for people to hang on to hurts, to suffer regrets, to imprison themselves in fear, to bear the pain of guilt. It's natural, too, to see a layer of fog hovering over the ocean in the morning. If the fog is heavy enough—and it often is along coastal areas—you can't see very far ahead of you. If you're out in the water, you can easily lose your bearings.

Perhaps you've woken up to the lowing of fog horns warning boats of high rocks and shallow water. Even a thin layer of fog over the water blurs sea and sky. And you might have noticed something else that's natural: The sun rises and burns off the fog. Now you can see the horizon. Now you can safely swim or sail.

Though the sun burns off coastal fog naturally, there's no natural way to burn off the fog of hurt, regret, fear, and guilt. Many people try various things to crawl out from under spiritual gloom, but natural responses do nothing to dissipate the fog. In fact, anger, denial, and worry only serve to thicken it. Jesus, the Son of God, alone has the power to burn off those things that burden your heart and spirit. Only he can lift the spiritual fog that keeps you from seeing your way to healthy and wholesome relationships, to bold, productive, and joyous living, to faith in the redemption he has won for you.

If you sense a spiritual fog descending over your soul, turn to spiritual Son-shine. Replace the lowing of negative thoughts with the clear call of God's holy Word. Trade the murkiness of fear for the clarity of his promises. Let go of the shadows of the past and freely step into the brightness of today. Yes, the Son burns away fog. Jesus heals. It's not natural; it's supernatural—and the most natural thing in the world to happen to you, a child of God.

"I will restore you to health and heal your wounds," declares the LORD.
Jeremiah 30:17

This is what the LORD says, ... "I will heal my people and will let them enjoy abundant peace and security."
Jeremiah 33:2, 6

No one ever looks in vain
to the Great Physician.
F. F. Bosworth

Dear Lord: I've tried to put the past behind me, to find a way over, under, around, or through old wounds and pain that have been with me for as long as I can remember. Heal me, I pray. Restore me to health— physically, mentally, emotionally, and spiritually. Do for me what I can't do for myself, and I'll praise you all my days. Amen.

Jesus Comes Running

QUIET, SECLUDED BEACHES have been your haven
through long, sleepy days. But today you decide to do
some people watching where the crowds are—at the swimming beach. Families troop in with their armloads of paraphernalia:
towels, coolers, inflatable toys, plastic buckets, and shovels for
building sand castles. Dad carries the heavy things; Mom carries her
own load, plus the numerous items kids deposit in her arms as they
dash for the water. Like a walking coatrack, you chuckle to yourself.

The lifeguard has his hands full today too. You shade your
eyes and peer up at the tall stand where he sits as a vigilant sentry,
scanning the waves. Most people think of life guarding as just a
summer job, and a pretty leisurely one at that, but when you think
about it, you can't help but admire the heroism.

What's notable is the way lifeguards keep watch. They aren't
just there to leap to the rescue in an emergency. They stay keenly
aware from their perches and whistle warnings to unwary swimmers
who are in potential danger, really looking out for their welfare.

Jesus is an awesome lifeguard! He shepherds over us all the
time. And he doesn't just grab us if we fall into the clutches of
trouble or get caught in the trap of sin. His mercy goes much further than that. He keeps a close watch over everything that
concerns us, and if we're listening, we'll hear him cautioning us
long before we've wandered too close to danger.

If we ignore his warnings and run headlong into harm's way

anyhow, his mercy still prevails. Never does he sit back and shake his head disapprovingly. No, Jesus comes running. Mercy rescues us as soon as we call out to him; in fact, I suspect he's on his way long before he hears our cry. Because, like the lifeguard in his tower, Jesus has been watching every moment.

> *The LORD your God is a merciful God; he will not abandon*
> *or destroy you or forget the covenant with your forefathers,*
> *which he confirmed to them by oath.*
> Deuteronomy 4:31

> *The Mighty One has done great things for me—holy is his name.*
> *His mercy extends to those who fear him,*
> *from generation to generation.*
> Luke 1:49–50

> GOD GIVETH HIS WRATH BY WEIGHT,
> *but* WITHOUT WEIGHT HIS MERCY.
> *Sir Thomas Fuller*

Dear God: I reach out for your mercy. I hold on to it as for my very life—for it is. Without your mercy, I'm lost, for I can never save myself. I'm wholly dependent on you. I know though, Lord, that I need not fear. Your mercy is well known and often noted in your Word. Teach me to show mercy to others as you've shown mercy to me. Amen.

Learning to Be Still

CONDITIONS ARE RIGHT. The water is calm in the protected bay. You pull rubbery fins onto your feet and flip-flop to the water's edge, looking and feeling very much like a duck, but hoping to transform into a graceful swan once you submerge. Mask defogged and snorkel strapped securely in place, you begin your adventure.

At first you swim along the surface and observe the underwater world as a polite visitor. Then, intrigued by a colorful cluster of sea life below, you take a deep gulp of air and dive down for a closer look.

It takes conscious thought, at this point, not to expend a lot of effort. You know that it's very important to be relaxed in order to stretch your time below—and to descend more quickly.

It's an amazing truth that an attitude of quietness and rest equips us to do almost anything more efficiently. As Christians, we perform God's will far more effectively when we simply trust him than when we strain and strive. In fact, his Word instructs us to rest in him, to wait patiently for him, never to fret or be anxious about anything.

While Martha bustled in fevered activity during Jesus' visit to their house, it was her sister, Mary, whom he commended, sitting quietly at his feet in worshipful silence, listening (Luke 10:38–42).

Rest is a high priority to God. He modeled it by

resting on the seventh day after creation, and he included it in the Ten Commandments.

Human nature tries to achieve by working harder; it's difficult for us to honor God's instruction to rest. Let the weight of his wisdom sink deep into your soul. Let him teach you the awesome, hidden power of rest.

My people will live in peaceful dwelling places, in secure homes, in undisturbed places of rest.
Isaiah 32:18

The beloved of the LORD rests in safety—the High God surrounds him all day long—the beloved rests between his shoulders.
Deuteronomy 33:12 NRSV

RENEWAL AND RESTORATION ARE NOT LUXURIES. THEY ARE ESSENTIALS. BEING ALONE AND RESTING FOR A WHILE IS NOT SELFISH. IT *is* CHRISTLIKE. TAKING YOUR DAY OFF EACH WEEK OR REWARDING YOURSELF WITH A RELAXING, REFRESHING VACATION IS NOT CARNAL. IT'S SPIRITUAL.
Charles R. Swindoll

Heavenly Father: Thank you for the rest that comes from knowing you, trusting you, obeying you. Even in the midst of my busy daily life, I know I can rest from anxiety because you are completely trustworthy. You can do so much more than I can do with all my striving. Take my burdens, carry my cares—I give them to you and receive in return a rest that can't be disturbed. Amen.

Safety in Numbers

How GOOD IT FEELS to get away from it all, to experience sweet solitude on the beach. You relish the hours that stretch before you and feel thankful for those that lie behind.

Life was tumbling in too fast, and it's been a real relief to set yourself apart, slow down, and spend time relaxing. You can just feel peace taking hold. You're even thinking more clearly.

Going back home will be a major readjustment. It takes a lot of energy just dealing with people on a daily basis. Still, you feel you'll be ready for that. After all, we were made for community.

You've been fascinated during your long walks at low tide by the many interesting sea animals you've observed. And you've noticed how they congregate. Scientists have studied this tendency, and they have a name for it: aggregation.

What they've discovered is that clustering into groups gives animals several advantages. Clumped together, anemones, corals, and other colonizing creatures are better protected against oxygen suffocation as well as water loss.

One of the most interesting discoveries is that the act of aggregating actually produces a protective substance—almost like an antibody—that helps the group resist poisons from predators.

Though you do need time alone, as a believer you're also meant to draw strength from other Christians. The writer of Hebrews offered this reminder: "Let us not give up meeting together, as some are in the habit of doing, but let us encourage one another" (10:25).

We need one another; none of us were meant to walk through this life all alone. God designed us to function as parts of a body so that when one of us is weak another can help.

It's good to be aware of when you need to get away and spend time renewing your spirit with God alone; it's also good to know when it's time to rejoin the family. There is safety, and strength, in numbers.

> The LORD gives strength to his people; the LORD
> blesses his people with peace.
> Psalm 29:11

Two are better than one, because they have a good reward for their toil. For if they fall, one will lift up the other; but woe to one who is alone and falls and does not have another to help.
Ecclesiastes 4:9–10 NRSV

NO MAN IS AN ISLAND, ENTIRE OF ITSELF;
EVERY MAN IS A PIECE *of* THE CONTINENT,
A PART OF THE MAIN.
John Donne

Dear Father: Thank you for the strength I gain from being with your people. I feel it every time we're together. I go away renewed in my faith and encouraged to continue walking closely with you in this dimly lit world. Show me how to do my part to strengthen others with kind words, constant prayers, and selfless caring. Amen.

We're All in the Same Boat

At the boat landing you're a delighted bystander while a patient father instructs his teenage daughter on steering a motorboat. Obviously a novice to all things nautical, she steps uncertainly into the boat, holding an arm up for balance as her father helps her get situated. But once behind the wheel, she seems to feel she's an expert.

Having recently learned to drive a car (she makes a point of that!), she expects to have no problem steering away from the dock into the channel, and she starts turning the wheel sharply that direction. Problem is, a fairly stiff breeze is blowing from the same direction, and, as Dad explains, her technique is likely to damage the propeller. She sighs, straightens the wheel, and not waiting to be further enlightened, tries going straight ahead instead.

Clunk, clunk, clunk! The boat bounces nearly the whole length of the dock before clearing it. You hear Dad's exasperated voice as they head jerkily toward the open water. "What you needed to do, hon, was shift into reverse, turn the wheel toward the dock, and ..."

But now she's embarrassed and only wants to get away from amused onlookers (yourself among them) standing innocently by, chuckling to themselves.

Oh, the lessons of humility. Teenage girls aren't the only ones who have to learn it. Funny how trying to look graceful or competent at anything before you actually are makes you do stupid things.

We all come to places where we realize how little we know compared to what we thought we knew. Pride is laid low, and if we submit ourselves to God's patient teaching, we go on a little wiser—and humbler.

But if we resist, convinced of our self-sufficiency, pretending we have it all together, our weaknesses will still be revealed. We just won't learn as much.

Humility is being willing to look a little silly at times. "Be completely humble and gentle," Scripture admonishes (Eph. 4:2). Take your inadequacies with good humor and don't be afraid to accept instruction from your gracious, patient Father.

Humility and the fear of the LORD bring wealth and honor and life.
Proverbs 22:4

*ℱ*OR THOSE WHO WOULD LEARN GOD'S WAYS, HUMILITY IS *the* FIRST THING, HUMILITY IS THE SECOND, HUMILITY IS THE THIRD.
Saint Augustine of Hippo

Heavenly Father: Forgive me for running ahead of you, confident that I know how to manage my life on my own. In trying to appear wise, I looked foolish. I've learned my lesson. Show me how to humble myself before you in every area of my life. Only then will I be able to please you. Amen.

The Art of Gleaning

THE MIDMORNING SEA IS ALIVE with bright, small ripples—"sun pennies," you've heard them called. The air is not windy, not still. Just right.

A group of grade-school students and their enthusiastic young teacher are here for a "seining" outing. Two children demonstrate the technique for the others. One at each end of a long rectangular net, they carry it above the water, walking out from shore, then drop and drag it toward the beach.

"Ooh's" and "aah's" abound as the students examine the thrilling, live aquatic loot. Assorted critters scramble, flap, and skitter in every direction. Little fingers poke, then pull back, careful not to get caught in the snapping claws of crabs and crawdads.

The teacher diligently helps the children sort and sift quickly so that nothing remains ashore long enough to endanger its survival. A few classroom aquarium specimens are kept. The rest are returned safely to their ocean home.

"Gather a lot ... glean a little," you muse as you walk down the beach. It's much like that in daily spiritual disciplines. Read the Bible faithfully, taking in truth by the pageful, and God sorts out the gems. Spend regular time with believers, and sweet fellowship deepens into a few special friendships. Listen to the preaching of God's Word, and the Spirit brings fresh insight.

Enjoy digging into God's Word; savor your time with Christian brothers and sisters; take in spiritual instruction. These are your "seine" of inspiration, packed with treasures just waiting to be sorted.

The path of the righteous is like the first gleam of dawn, shining ever brighter till the full light of day.
Proverbs 4:18

If you call out for insight and cry aloud for understanding, and if you look for it as for silver and search for it as for hidden treasure, then you will understand the fear of the LORD and find the knowledge of God.
Proverbs 2:3-5

LOOK AT THE LIVES OF THOSE MEN AND THE TIME THEY GAVE TO SCRIPTURE READING AND PRAYER AND VARIOUS OTHER FORMS OF SELF-EXAMINATION AND SPIRITUAL EXERCISES. THEY BELIEVED *in* ... THE DISCIPLINE OF THE SPIRITUAL LIFE AND ... GOD REWARDED THEM BY GIVING THEM GRACIOUS MANIFESTATIONS OF HIMSELF AND MIGHTY EXPERIENCES WHICH WARMED THEIR HEARTS.
Martyn Lloyd-Jones

Heavenly Father: Thank you for the inspiration I gain from the resources you've placed in my life. As I walk in obedience to you, open my eyes to see and my ears to hear those inspiring nuggets of truth that will help me along the way. Amen.

The Lasting Kind

The ocean shore at dusk is a romantic setting for people in love. Deep colors interplay between sand and sky, dressing the gleaming water in mysterious, sequined evening wear.

Couples walk side by side, and the brisk air naturally calls for an arm around the shoulder. You watch a young pair of lovers playfully write their names in the sand, share a kiss, then walk off hand in hand, her head resting on his shoulder.

It's a sight that's both happy and a little sad. They must love to imagine that their young romantic excitement will last forever, as we all do. We spend blissful hours building elaborate sand castles to house our dreams, only to find that all too often the tide of real life washes them away.

A song called "Written in the Sand" sets such a scene. "Thought I'd found the secret to painting dreams with yesterday's smiles / Then I watched the waves rush in where our footsteps ran," laments the lyric. Nothing symbolizes impermanence quite like the seashore, washed relentlessly clean by the tide each day.

The temporary nature of our human passions has both its positive and negative aspects. On the downside is the almost inevitable heartbreak and loss we experience when our fickle relationships change, die, or fall apart. The good news is that because our hearts are changeable, we have the ability to let time heal wounds. Forgiveness washes away wrongs done. People move on, hearts mend, and even the most brokenhearted can learn to love again.

Isn't it good to know that Christ has a love for us that will never fade? His love is both deeper and longer lasting than any we can experience or imagine between human beings. It's wide enough to encompass all our pain and high enough to contain our greatest joys! Jesus' love lasts forever. Be blessed by loving in return a Savior who wants to spend eternity with you!

As high as the heavens are above the earth,
so great is [God's] love for those who fear him.
Psalm 103:11

God so loved the world that he gave his only Son, so that everyone
who believes in him may not perish but may have eternal life.
John 3:16 NRSV

GOD CREATED MAN BECAUSE GOD LOVES
AND WANTED *an* OBJECT TO LOVE. HE CREATED
MAN SO THAT HE COULD RETURN HIS LOVE.
Billy Graham

Oh, Lord: The Bible says that you love me—tirelessly, completely. My mind can't take in such a wonderful and unexplainable truth, but my heart takes hold without hesitation. Expand my heart to love you even more. Amen.

Accept No Substitutes

IT'S A BEAUTIFUL EVENING. The sea is calm and translucent, pearly as the inside of a shell, barely moving. You wonder, as you stand there mesmerized by its soft, lulling motion, if beneath the surface it's indeed as calm as it seems.

You know that underneath the peaceful rhythm of the waves washing gently onto shore, there's something called current, the back and forth, horizontal movement of the sea resulting from the tide and other factors. And you know that although the current is strongest in deep water, it can also present a hidden danger to swimmers.

Sometimes referred to as riptides, the more accurately named rip currents can be deceptive. The ocean can seem harmlessly still, yet one of these currents can catch you unaware and suddenly pull you along in its very strong force.

In the same way, we as Christians sometimes attempt to mask our unrest when we're caught up in negative emotions—such as fear, anger, or anxiety—while inwardly our peace is being ripped away. We don't want others to know about our inner turmoil, so we use all our energy to conceal it instead of simply asking for prayer and support. The appearance of peacefulness we present is a false peace, not the true kind Christ gives.

The thing about rip currents is that they need not be of any real danger if you know what to do when caught in one. If you swim parallel to the shore until the pull stops, you can then swim back safely or tread water and wave for lifeguard assistance.

It's always safer to be honest about your struggles, admit them, and ask for prayer. The Lord promises to come to your aid, bringing with him genuine peace.

"Though the mountains be shaken
and the hills be removed,
yet my unfailing love for you will not be shaken
nor my covenant of peace be removed,"
says the LORD, *who has compassion on you.*
Isaiah 54:10

I will lie down and sleep in peace,
for you alone, O LORD,
make me dwell in safety.
Psalm 4:8

PEACE IS NOT THE ABSENCE OF CONFLICT BUT THE
PRESENCE OF GOD, *no* MATTER WHAT THE CONFLICT.
Author Unknown

Dear Lord: Your peace sustains me, strengthens me, comforts me, and nourishes me even in the midst of this troubled world. It follows me wherever I go. Thank you for the peace that can't be measured or understood. You are a good and gracious God. Amen.

The Pearl of Great Price

I't's MIDAFTERNOON AND THE SEA BREEZE is soothing. You stir drowsily after drifting comfortably in and out of sleep. Your eyes skip lazily over the variety of shells scattered along the beach. Smiling to yourself, you allow your mind to fantasize: *You reach out your hand to pick up a nearby shell and find a priceless pearl inside.*

If only pearls were that easy to obtain. In reality, pearl diving is a difficult and risky pursuit. Competition is fierce, and only one in thousands of mollusks may yield the coveted prize. Repeated dives into deep water not only present hazards to the body—decompression sickness ("the bends"), burst eardrums, and the strain of pure exhaustion—but divers also face the danger of being attacked by marine creatures, such as sharks, stingrays, and moray eels. Still, the promise of the reward keeps their efforts alive.

Jesus, when he was nailed to the cross, endured unspeakable pain and suffering "for the joy set before him" (Heb. 12:2). Like a pearl of great price, he focused not on the cost but on the end result of bringing precious souls into right relationship with God. Our eternal life is Christ's pearl of great price. When Jesus finds a heart devoted to him, he rejoices over us with singing (Zeph. 3:17)!

Like the widow in the parable of the lost coin (Luke 15:8–10), we've all felt the great relief and happiness of finding a lost object we value. How much more intensely must our loving Creator-God feel joy when one of his children draws near to him.

Remember how willingly he suffered to redeem you. Never forget how valuable you are to him.

Be glad and rejoice forever in what I will create, for I will create Jerusalem to be a delight and its people a joy. I will rejoice over Jerusalem and take delight in my people; the sound of weeping and of crying will be heard in it no more.

Isaiah 65:18–19

Maidens will dance and be glad, young men and old as well. I will turn their mourning into gladness; I will give them comfort and joy instead of sorrow.

Jeremiah 31:13

When I think upon my God, my heart is so full of joy that the notes dance and leap from my pen; and since God has given me a cheerful heart, it will be pardoned me that I serve him with a cheerful spirit.

Franz Joseph Haydn

Precious Father: I will never know why you love me, why you want me, why you gave so much to redeem me and adopt me as your own child. But I thank you for it. And I thank you for the opportunity it gives me to have a personal relationship with you—the great God of all creation. I will seek that relationship with all my heart. I will make it my greatest priority in life. I will seek you as a precious pearl, even though no pearl could ever compare with you. Amen.

A Wellspring of Life

TODAY ISN'T A STILL, QUIET, lying-in-the-sun day. A strong wind running parallel to the shoreline tugs at trees, bends tall grass sideways, whips waves into a churning, energetic dance, and sends clouds skidding speedily across the sky. Still, you'd rather go out walking than watch all this excitement from indoors, so you pull on a jacket and venture out onto the beach.

The ocean is busy today—busy being renewed.

Upwelling is a term used to describe a phenomenon that's important to the life of the ocean. Currents flow along the coastline, combining with wind patterns and the earth's rotation to deflect surface water away from shore. As this shallow, warmer water is pulled out to sea, it's replaced by cold water welling up from below.

This is highly beneficial because the deep, dense water that's pumped to the surface by these strong winds carries with it minerals that are rich in nutrients. They foster the growth of plants, in turn enriching the entire ocean population of fish and countless other sea creatures, supporting the whole food chain.

The word upwelling is sometimes used in other ways, such as describing a buildup of emotional passion or a gathering of strength and fortitude.

In your spiritual life, the Lord sees when you need replenishing, and in his tireless work of renewal, he uses a process similar to upwelling. His renewal process strengthens you. He sweeps away your shallow waters, lifeless and lukewarm, then floods your inner being with rich, abundant waters that spring from the very depths of his life-giving wellspring.

Many times it can be painful, even grievous, to succumb to this process, letting go of the old and comfortable to make way for the new. But the Spirit's regenerating power enables change to take place in your heart in order to revitalize and prepare you for greater things.

Be glad for the cleansing upwelling God brings. Let him replenish your spirit and refresh your soul.

> *Though outwardly we are wasting away, yet inwardly*
> *we are being renewed day by day.*
> 2 Corinthians 4:16

I ... LIKE SUNRISES, MONDAYS,
AND NEW SEASONS. GOD SEEMS TO BE SAYING,
"WITH ME YOU CAN ALWAYS START AFRESH."
Ada Lum

Dear Father: Thank you for your renewing work that is constantly going on in my heart and mind. Not only do you receive me just as I am, but you clean me up and make me holy and beautiful in your sight. I love you, Lord, and I'll love you more each and every day. You make me so much more than I could ever be without you. Amen.

Topical Index

Additional copies of this and other products from Honor Books
are available from your local bookseller.

Also available from Honor Books:

Mountain Prayers: A Vacation for Your Soul

If you have enjoyed this book, or if it has had an impact
on your life, we would like to hear from you.

Please contact us at

Honor Books, Dept. 201
4050 Lee Vance View
Colorado Springs, CO 80918

Or visit our Web site
www.cookministries.com

HONOR HB BOOKS

Inspiration and Motivation for the Seasons of Life